HH

sh
bo
t
'

R
Fi
ir
b

THE GOURMET

THE
GOURMET

MURIEL BARBERY

*Translated from the French
by Alison Anderson*

Gallic Books
London

A Gallic Book

First published in France as *Une gourmandise* by
Éditions Gallimard, Paris

Copyright © Éditions Gallimard, Paris, 2000
English translation copyright © Europa Editions 2009

First published in Great Britain in 2009 by
Gallic Books, 134 Lots Road, London SW10 0RJ

A CIP record for this book is available from the British Library

ISBN 978-1-906040-26-0

Typeset by
SX Composing DTP, Rayleigh, Essex

Printed and bound by
CPI Mackays, Chatham, Kent, ME5 8TD

To Stéphane, without whom . . .

CONTENTS

Flavour

Rue de Grenelle, the Bedroom

When I took possession of the table, it was as supreme monarch. We were kings, the suns of those few hours of banqueting, who would determine their futures and describe their horizons – tragically limited or mouth-wateringly distant and radiant – as chefs. I would stride into the room the way a consul entered the arena, and I would give the order for the feast to begin. Those who have never tasted the intoxicating nectar of power cannot imagine the sudden explosion of adrenalin that radiates throughout the body, releasing a harmony of movement, erasing all fatigue, along with any reality that does not bend to the orders of your pleasure; the ecstasy of unbridled power, when one need no longer struggle but merely enjoy the spoils of battle, and savour without cease the headiness that comes from inspiring fear.

That is who we were, and how we reigned as lords and masters over the finest establishments in France, filled with the excellence of the dishes, with our own glory and with our unquenchable desire – like a hunting dog's first, excited flair – to pronounce upon that excellence.

I am the greatest food critic in the world. It is I who have taken this minor art and raised it to a rank of utmost prestige. Everyone knows my name, from Paris to Rio, Moscow to Brazzaville, Saigon to Melbourne and Acapulco. I have made and unmade reputations, and at sumptuous banquets I have been the knowing and merciless *maître d'œuvre,* expediting to the four corners of the globe the salt or honey of my pen, in newspapers and broadcasts and various forums, to which I have repeatedly been invited to discourse upon that which previously had been reserved for a few select specialist journals or intermittent weekly columns. I have, for all eternity, pinned to my list of discoveries some of the most prestigious butter-flies among practising chefs. The glory and the demise of Partais, or the fall of Sangerre, or the increasingly incandescent success of Marquet can be attributed to me alone. For all eter-nity, indeed, I have made them what they are; for all eternity.

I have held eternity under the skin of my words, and tomorrow I shall die. I shall die in forty-eight hours – unless I have been dying for sixty-eight years and it is only today that I have deigned to notice. Whatever the case may be, the sentence was handed down yesterday by my friend the physician Chabrot: 'Old boy, you've got forty-eight hours.' How ironic! After decades of nosh, deluges of wine and alcohol of every sort, after a life spent in butter, cream, rich sauces and oil in con-stant, knowingly orchestrated and meticulously cajoled excess, my trustiest right-hand men, Sir Liver and his associate Stomach, are doing marvellously well and it is my heart that is giving out. I am dying of heart failure. What a bitter pill to swallow! So often have I reproached others for a lack of heart in their cuisine, in their art, that never for a moment did I think that I might be the one lacking therein, this heart now betraying me so brutally, with scarcely concealed disdain, so quickly has the blade been sharpened . . .

I am going to die, but that is of no importance. Since yesterday, since Chabrot, only one thing matters. I am going to die and there is a flavour that has been teasing my taste buds and my heart and I simply cannot recall it. I know that this particular flavour is the first and ultimate truth of my entire life, and that it holds the key to a heart that I have since silenced. I know that it is a flavour from childhood or adolescence, an original, marvellous dish that predates my vocation as a critic, before I had any desire or pretension to expound on my pleasure in eating. A forgotten flavour, lodged in my deepest self, and which has surfaced in the twilight of my life as the only truth ever told – or realised. I search, and cannot find.

(Renée)

Rue de Grenelle, the Concierge's Lodge

And now what?

Is it not enough for them that every day the Good Lord gives us I clean up the muck that falls from their rich people's shoes, I vacuum the dust they stir up during their rich people's deambulations, I listen to their rich people's conversations and concerns, I feed their doggies, their kitties, water their plants, wipe the noses of their offspring, accept their yearly gifts of money – and that is indeed the only moment when they don't play at being rich – I sniff their perfume, I open the door to their relatives, I hand out their post dripping with bank statements regarding their rich people's accounts and investments and overdrafts, I force myself to smile in response to their rich people's smiles, and, finally, I live in their rich people's building, me, the concierge, a total nobody, a thing behind a window, that people say hello to in great haste to ease their conscience, because it's awkward, isn't it, to see that old thing lurking in her dark little hole without crystal chandeliers, without patent leather shoes, without a camelhair coat, it's awkward but at the same time it's reassuring, like some incarnation of the social differences that justify the superiority of their class, like an ugly thing exalting their munificence, like a foil enhancing their elegance – no, all that is not enough, because in addition to all that, in addition to leading this existence as an unbecoming recluse day after day, hour after hour, minute after minute, and what's worst of all, year after year, I am expected to *understand* their rich people's sorrows?

If they want to have news of the Maître, let them ring *his* bell.

14

The Man of Property

Rue de Grenelle, the Bedroom

If I go back to my earliest memories, I find that I have always liked eating. I cannot pinpoint exactly my first gastronomic ecstasies, but there is no doubt as to the identity of my first preferred cook: my own grandmother. On the menu for celebrations there was meat in gravy, potatoes in gravy, and the wherewithal to mop up all that gravy. I never knew, subsequently, whether it was my childhood or the stews themselves that I was unable to re-experience, but never again have I sampled as fervently (I am a specialist in that oxymoron) as at my grandmother's table the likes of those potatoes: bursting with gravy, delectable little sponges. Might the forgotten taste throbbing in my breast be hidden somewhere in there? Might it suffice to ask Anna to let a few tubers marinate in the juices of a good traditional coq au vin? Alas, I know only too well that it would not. I know that what I am searching for is something that has always eluded my talents, my memory, my consideration. Extravagant pots-au-feu, chicken chasseur to make one faint, dizzying coqs au vin, astounding blanquettes – you have all been the companions of my carnivorous and saucy childhood. I cherish you, amiable casseroles with your fragrance of game – but you are not what I am seeking at this moment.

Despite those early, always faithful, love affairs, in later years my tastes turned to other culinary destinations, and with the additional delight occasioned by the certainty of my own eclecticism, my love of stew came to be replaced by the urgent call of more austere sensations. The soft, delicate touch on the palate of one's first sushi no longer holds any secrets for me, and I bless the day my tongue discovered the intoxicating, almost erotic, velvet-smooth caress of an oyster slipping in after a chunk of bread smeared with salted butter. I have dissected the magical delicacy of the oyster with such brilliance and finesse that the divine mouthful has become a religious act for all. Between these two extremes – the rich warmth of a daube and the clean crystal of shellfish – I have covered the entire range of culinary art, for I am an encyclopedic aesthete who is always one dish ahead of the game – but always one heart behind.

I can hear Paul and Anna speaking in hushed voices in the corridor. I peer through my eyelids. My gaze, as usual, encounters the perfect curve of a sculpture by Fanjol, a birthday present from Anna on my sixtieth birthday; it seems such a long time ago. Paul comes quietly into the room. Of all my nephews and nieces, he is the only one I love and respect, the only one whose presence I can tolerate during the final hours of my life. Therefore, before I can no longer speak at all, I have taken him – along with my wife – into my confidence regarding my distress.

'A dish? A dessert?' asked Anna, with a sob in her voice.

I cannot bear to see her like this. I love my wife, as I have always loved the beautiful objects in my life. That is the way it is. I have lived as a man of property, and I shall die as one, with neither qualms nor sentimental indulgence; nor do I regret having accumulated property or having conquered souls and beings as if I were acquiring an expensive painting. A work of art has a soul. It cannot be reduced to a simple mineral existence, to the lifeless elements of which it consists. Perhaps because I know this I have never felt the least bit ashamed of considering Anna the most beautiful work of all – this woman who for forty years has used her finely chiselled beauty and her dignified tenderness to enliven the chambers of my realm.

I do not like to see her cry. On the threshold of death, I feel that she is waiting for something, that she suffers for the imminent end looming on the horizon of the coming hours, and that she is dreading I might disappear into the same void, bereft of communication, that we have maintained since our wedding – it is the same void, but definitive now, without appeal or hope, the false promises that tomorrow will, perhaps, be another day. I know that she is thinking or feeling all of this, but that is not what worries me. We have nothing to say to each other, she and I, and she will have to accept that things are just as I have wished them. All I want is for her to understand that that is the way it is, to appease her suffering and, above all, my displeasure.

Nothing except that flavour I am pursuing in the limbo of my memory is of any importance now: enraged by a betrayal I cannot even recall, it continues to resist me, and stubbornly slips away.

Rue de Grenelle, the Stairway

I remember our holidays in Greece when we were children, on Tinos – a horrid island, bare and scorched, that I hated from the moment I saw it, from the moment we set foot on solid ground, from the moment we left the gangplank of the ship, the moment we left the winds of the Aegean behind . . .

A big grey and white cat had leapt onto the terrace and from there onto the low wall that separated our villa from the neighbours' invisible house. A big cat: by the standards of the country, he was impressive. The neighbourhood abounded in scrawny creatures with bobbing heads and it broke my heart to see them dragging their exhausted bodies around. This cat, however, seemed to have grasped the principles of survival: he had made it past the terrace, got as far as the door to the dining room, and once inside the house had grown bold and shamelessly swept down like some avenging angel upon the roast chicken that was resting in state upon the table. We found him comfortably indulging in our victuals, not the least bit intimidated, or perhaps just enough to enchant, in the time it took to grab a wing with a smart, expert snap of his teeth and to sneak off through the French doors, his loot in his chops, with a perfunctory growl to our great childish delight.

Of course, *he* wasn't there. He would be coming back from Athens a few days later, and we'd tell him the story – Maman would tell him the story, oblivious to his scornful expression, his absence of love – he would pay no attention, he already had his mind on his next feast, far away, at the ends of the earth –

without us. All the same, he would look at me with a glint of disappointment in the depths of his eyes, unless it was repulsion, or perhaps cruelty – perhaps all three at the same time – and say, 'That is how to survive, that cat is a living lesson,' and his words would ring like a bell, words meant to hurt, words meant to wound, to torture the frightened little girl I was, so weak and insignificant: of no importance.

He was a brutal man. Brutal in his gestures, in the dominating way he had of grabbing hold of things, his smug laugh, his raptor's gaze. I never saw him *relax*: everything was a pretext for tension. Already at breakfast, on those rare days when he deigned to grace us with his presence, our martyrdom began. The stage was set for psychodrama, he would splutter and expostulate: for the survival of the Empire was at stake, what were we having for lunch? Trips to the market were opportunities for hysteria. My mother bowed to his will, as usual, as always. And then off he would go again, to other restaurants, other women, other holidays, without us, where we were not even – of this I am sure – cause for memories; perhaps, just, as he was leaving, we were like flies to him, unwanted flies that you brush away with a sweep of your hand so you needn't think about them any more. We were his coleopterous insects.

It was one evening; he was walking ahead of us, past the little tourist boutiques in Tinos's only shopping street, with his imperious gait, his hands in his pockets, mindful of no one. The earth could have collapsed beneath our feet, it was all the same to him; he strode ahead and it was up to our little terrorised children's legs to close the chasm between us. We did not yet know that this was the last holiday he would spend with us. The following summer it was with relief – with frenzied delight – that we greeted the news that he wouldn't be coming with us. But we quickly had to resign ourselves to another affliction, that of Maman wandering like a ghost through the places we were meant to enjoy. It struck us as worse than ever because by his very absence he managed to hurt us even more. But on the day I'm remembering, he was very much present and he was climbing up the hill at a discouraging rate – I had just stopped outside a humble little neon-lit restaurant with my hand to my waist, plagued by a cramp. My sides heaving, I was trying to catch my breath when I saw with terror that he was making his way back down to me, followed by Jean, who was livid and gazing at me with big tearful eyes; I stopped breathing. He walked by without seeing me, strode into the little greasy spoon, greeted the proprietor, and while we stood uncertainly on the threshold, hopping from one foot to the other, he pointed to something behind the counter, raised a hand with his fingers well spread to indicate 'three', and motioned briefly to us to enter as he made his way to a table at the far side of the bar.

They were *loukoumades*, perfectly round little fritters that are dropped into boiling oil just long enough for the outside to become crisp while the inside stays tender and cottony; they are then covered in honey and served very hot on a little plate, with a fork and a tall glass of water. You see, nothing changes. I think the way he does. Just like him, I dissect each sensation in succession; like him, I cloak them with adjectives, dilate them, stretch them over the length of a sentence, or a verbal melody, and I let nothing of the actual food remain, only these magician's words, which will make the readers believe they have been eating as we did . . . Not for nothing am I his daughter . . .

He tasted a fritter, made a face, pushed his plate back and watched us. Although I couldn't see him I sensed that Jean, next to me, was having a terrible time swallowing; whereas I was postponing the moment when I would have to take another bite and, petrified, I gave him a stupid look, for he was studying us.

'Do you like them?' he asked, in his grating voice.

Panic and disorientation. Next to me Jean was breathing quietly. I forced myself.

'Yes,' I muttered timidly.

'Why?' he pursued, his tone increasingly dry, but I could see that in the depth of his eyes, which were actually inspecting me for the first time in years, there was a new spark, something I had never seen, like a little speck of cautious anticipation and hope, inconceivable, harrowing and paralysing, because for so long I had been accustomed to his not expecting a thing from me.

'Because it's good?' I ventured, hunching my shoulders.

I had lost. How many times since then have I relived in my mind – and in images – this wrenching episode, the moment when something could have shifted, when the bleakness of my fatherless childhood might have been transformed into a new and brilliant love . . . As if in slow motion, against the painful backdrop of my disappointed desire, the seconds tick by; the question, the answer, the waiting, and then the annihilation. The gleam in his eyes is extinguished as quickly as it flared. Disgusted, he turns away, pays, and I am once again relegated to the solitary confinement of his indifference.

But what am I doing here on these stairs, with my pounding heart, rehashing these horrible memories I left behind so long ago – or which should have been left behind, should have subsided after so many years of necessary suffering on my analyst's couch, of being attentive to my own words and conquering each day a bit more of the right to be something other than hatred and terror, the right just to be myself. Laura. His daughter . . . No. I won't go. I've already mourned the father I didn't have.

Meat

Rue de Grenelle, the Bedroom

We left the ship amidst the crowds, noise, dust and general weariness. It had taken two exhausting days to cross Spain, but that was already nothing more than a ghost lingering on the frontier of memory. Sticky, worn out by miles of hazardous roads, displeased with the hasty roadside stops and the barely edible restaurant food, crushed by the heat in the crowded car, which was at last slowly making its way along the pier, we were still living for a short while longer in the world of travel, but already we could sense the splendour of arrival.

Tangiers. Where many a passage has ended and many a new journey has begun. With its vigorous port, its embarkations and disembarkations, perhaps the most powerful city on earth. Halfway between Madrid and Casablanca, it is a formidable town that, unlike Algeciras on the other side of the straits, has avoided becoming merely a port town. Consistent, instantly itself despite its piers gaping open onto elsewhere, an enclave of the senses at a crossroads, Tangiers instantly seized hold of us with its vigour. Our journey was nearly over. And although our final destination was Rabat, the town that was the cradle of my mother's family and where, since the return to France, we spent every summer, we always felt, as soon as we reached Tangiers, that we had arrived. We would park the car outside the Hotel Bristol, modest but clean, on a steep street that led to the medina. A shower and then later, on foot, we would make our way to the theatre of succulence foretold.

*

It was at the entrance to the medina. Arrayed beneath the arcades on the square, a number of small kebab restaurants greeted passers-by. We went into 'our' restaurant and went up to the second floor: a huge table took all the space in the narrow room whose walls were painted blue and which looked out over the circular piazza below; we would sit down, our stomachs tight and eager in anticipation of the unchanging set menu that was just waiting upon our pleasure. A pitiful but conscientious fan gave the room the charm of a breezy space but did little to refresh us; the harried waiter set down on the sticky Formica some glasses and a carafe of iced water. My mother would order in perfect Arabic. Scarcely five minutes passed before the dishes were there on the table.

Perhaps I shall not find what I am looking for. I will, at least, have had the opportunity to recall this: the grilled meat, the mechouia salad, the mint tea and the *cornes de gazelle*. I was Ali Baba. The cave of treasures: this was it, the perfect rhythm, the shimmering harmony between portions, each one exquisite unto itself, but verging on the sublime by virtue of the strict, ritual succession. The meatballs, grilled with the utmost respect for their firmness, had lost none of their succulence during their passage through fire, and filled my professionally carnivorous mouth with a thick, warm, spicy, juicy wave of masticatory pleasure. The sweet bell peppers, unctuous and fresh, softened my taste buds already subjugated by the virile rigour of the meat, and prepared them for the next powerful assault. Everything was there in abundance. From time to time we would take a sip of that carbonated water you can also find in Spain but which seems to have no real equivalent in France: a stinging, insolent, invigorating water, neither bland nor too bubbly. When at last, sated and somewhat dazed, we would shove our plates away and look in vain for a back to the bench so that we might relax, the waiter brought the tea, poured it according to the established ritual, and on

23

the table, which had been only haphazardly wiped clean, set down a plate of sugar-covered crescents, the *cornes de gazelle*. No one was the least bit hungry any more, but that is precisely what is so good about the moment devoted to pastries: they can only be appreciated to the full extent of their subtlety when they are not eaten to assuage our hunger, when the orgy of their sugary sweetness is not destined to fill some primary need but to coat our palate with all the benevolence of the world.

If my quest today is to lead me somewhere, no doubt it will not be far from this quintessence of civilisation, the extraordinary contrast between the pungency of a simple, powerful piece of meat and the knowing tenderness of a sweet and utterly superfluous delicacy. The entire history of humanity, of our tribe of sensitive predators, can be summed up in these meals in Tangiers, and in retrospect this is why they had such an uncommon power to exhilarate.

I shall never return to that beautiful maritime metropolis, where you arrive at the port, the long-hoped-for refuge during the storm – never again. But what do I care? I am on the road to my redemption. And it is far from the beaten path, along a road where the nature of our human condition can be truly felt, in a place far from the luxurious banquets of my career as a critic and the attendant prestige, that I must now seek the instrument of my salvation.

Rue de Provence

The first time was at Marquet's. You should have seen it,
you ought to have witnessed it at least once in your life
– the way this huge feline would take possession of the
room, his leonine majesty, the royal nod in greeting the maître
d', be it as a regular, a distinguished guest, or a proprietor. He
remains standing, almost in the middle of the room, conversing with Marquet, who has just come out of her den, the
kitchen; he places his hand on her shoulder as they make their
way to his table. There are many people around them, speaking loudly, they are all splendid with a combination of arrogance
and grace but you can tell that they are watching him on the sly,
that they are resplendent in his shadow, that they are hanging
on his every word. He is the Maître and, surrounded by the
stars of his retinue, he disposes, while they merely chatter.

The maître d' had to whisper in his ear, 'One of your young
colleagues is here today, sir.' He turned towards me, observed
me for a brief moment during which I felt as if I were being
X-rayed right through to my deepest mediocrities, and then he
turned away. Almost immediately I was summoned to join him
at his table.

It was a master class, one of those days when he donned the
robes of spiritual guide and invited all the finest young food
critics in Europe to dine with him, and like a pontiff gone back
to mere preaching, from the height of his pulpit he taught the
trade to a few bedazzled disciples. The Pope enthroned among

his cardinals: there was indeed something of a great cere-monial mass about this gastronomic council, where he reigned supreme over a hushed, contemplative elite. The rules were simple. You ate, you commented as you liked, he listened, sentence was passed. I was paralysed. Like an ambitious but shy fellow who is introduced for the first time to the Godfather, or a young man from the provinces at his first Parisian soirée; like a besotted admirer who encounters his Diva by chance, or a little shoemaker whose gaze meets that of the Princess, or a young author entering the temple of publish-ing for the first time: like them, I was petrified. He was the Christ and, at that particular Last Supper, I was Judas – not that I wanted to betray him, merely that I was an impostor, lost on Olympian heights, invited by mistake, and whose paltry blandness would, at any moment, be revealed in broad day-light. I was silent throughout the entire meal and he did not call upon me, keeping the whip or the caress of his decrees for his herd of regular followers. At dessert, however, he did question me, in silence. Everyone was commenting unsuccess-fully on a scoop of orange sorbet.

Unsuccessfully. All criteria are subjective. Something that when measured by common sense might seem magical and masterful will fracture pathetically when faced with the sheer rock face of genius. Their conversation was dizzying; the art of speaking supplanted the art of tasting. They all promised, to a man – by virtue of the mastery and precision of their commentary, and the dazzling skill of their practised tirades, which penetrated the sorbet with brilliant syntax and poetic flashes – to become masters of culinary expression one day, for if they were still in the shadow of their elder's aura, this would only be temporary. Meanwhile, the uneven, almost lumpy orange sphere continued to liquefy in our plates, its silent avalanche reflecting something of his disapproval. For nothing met with his approval.

Irritated, on the verge of extreme bad temper or even self-loathing for having allowed himself to be shackled with such pathetic company . . . his tenebrous gaze catches hold of mine, inviting me . . . I clear my throat, quaking and pink with confusion, because the sorbet does indeed inspire many things, but not the sort of things one ought to say here, at this concert of high-flying phraseologists, amidst these orchestra seats filled with culinary strategists, confronted with this living genius with his immortal pen and fiery eyes. And yet now I must – I must say something, and right away, because his entire person is emanating impatience and irritation. Therefore I clear my throat once again, moisten my lips, and step off into the void.

'It reminds me of the sorbets my grandmother used to make . . .'

On the face of the infatuated young man sitting across from me I see an incipient smile of mockery, his cheeks starting slowly to expand with the mirth that will explode into lethal laughter, and ready to give me a first-class burial: good evening, goodbye, dear sir, you came, don't come back again, a very good night to you.

But *he* is smiling at me with a warmth one would not have thought him capable of: a broad, frank smile, the smile of a wolf but intended from one wolf to another in the complicity of the pack, friendly, relaxed, something like, hello friend, it's good to find you here. And he says, 'So tell me, then, about your grandmother.'

It is an invitation, but also a veiled threat. While his request may seem kindly, it is weighted with the obligation for me to perform and the danger that after such a fine beginning I might disappoint him. My reply was a pleasant surprise to him, for it was in stark contrast to the bravura passages of the virtuoso soloists, and he liked that. For the time being.

'My grandmother's cooking . . .' I say, searching desperately for my words, for the decisive formula that will justify both my reply and my art – my talent.

But most unexpectedly he comes to my rescue.

'Would you believe' – and he smiles at me, almost affectionately – 'I also had a grandmother, whose kitchen was a magic cave for me. I think that my entire career sprang from the scents and aromas that came from that kitchen and which filled me, as a child, with desire. I literally went mad with desire. People don't really know what desire is, true desire, when it hypnotises you and takes hold of your entire soul, surrounds it utterly, in such a way that you become demented, possessed, ready to do anything for a tiny crumb, for a whiff of whatever is being concocted there beneath your nostrils, subjugated by the devil's own perfume! And my grandmother was overflowing with energy and a scathing good humour, a prodigious life force that suffused her entire kitchen with a sort of brilliant vitality, and it was as if I were at the heart of some molten matter: she radiated, and enveloped me in this warm and fragrant radiance!'

'With me, it was an impression rather of entering the temple,' I say, relieved, in possession now of the strength of my intuition and thus of my argumentation (I let out a long inward sigh). 'My grandmother was not so cheerful and radiant, far from it. She embodied rather the character of austere, sub-missive dignity. Protestant to the tips of her fingers, only ever cooking calmly and painstakingly, without passion or thrills, an affair of white porcelain platters and soup tureens that came to a table filled with silent guests, who without haste or visible emotion consumed dishes that could have made you burst with joy and delight.'

'How odd,' he says to me, 'I have always attributed the success and magic of her good-natured, tasty cooking to her easy temperament and southern sensuality. I even thought at times that it was her stupidity and lack of education and culture that had made her an accomplished cook, and that all the energy which did not nourish her mind was free to nourish her fare.'

'No,' I say after a moment's reflection, 'what went into their art was neither their personality nor their gift for life, any more than it was the simplicity of their spirit, their love of a job well done, or their austerity. I think they were aware, without even telling themselves as much, that they were accomplishing a noble task, one at which they could excel and that was subordinate, material or basely utilitarian in appearance only. They knew well enough that, beyond all the humiliations they had suffered not in their own name but by virtue of their condition as women, that when their men came home and sat down at the table, their own reign, as women, would begin. And it wasn't some sort of stranglehold they had over their "home economy", where they would, as sovereigns in their own right, take revenge on the power that the men had "abroad". It was a great deal more than that; they knew that their immense skill spoke directly to the hearts and the bodies of their men, and that in the eyes of those men this conferred upon the women a power greater than that which the women themselves attributed to male intrigues of power and money or all the compelling arguments of society. They held their men not by the ties of domestic administration, or of children or respectability or even those of the bedroom, but by their taste buds, and this was as sure a thing as if they had put them into a cage into which the men had rushed of their own volition.'

He is listening to me very attentively and I am learning to recognise in him the quality – so rare among men of power – that enables one to determine where display – the conversation allowing each participant to mark his territory and show signs of power – ends, and true dialogue begins. Around us, however, things are falling apart. The presumptuous young fellow who only a moment ago was so eager to assail me with

29

his mockery now has a waxy complexion and a vacant stare. The others remain silent, at the edge of an abyss of desolation. I continue.

'What did they feel, those men – so full of themselves, those "heads" of the family, trained from the dawn of time, in a patriarchal society, to become the masters – when they took their first bite of those simple yet extraordinary dishes that their wives had prepared in their private laboratories? What does a man experience when his tongue – which, up to this point, has been saturated with spices, sauces, meat, cream and salt – is suddenly refreshed by contact with a slow avalanche of ice and fruit that is ever so slightly rustic, and ever so slightly lumpy; thus, what was ephemeral is now slightly less so, slowed by the more sluggish deliquescence of fruity little chunks of ice gently breaking apart . . . Quite simply, those men experienced paradise, and even if they could not admit it to themselves, they knew very well that they were incapable of offering it to their wives in return, because for all their empires and arrogance, they could never make their women swoon the way those women made them swoon – with an orgasmic experience of the taste buds.'

He interrupts me without brutality.

'It's very interesting,' he says, 'I see exactly what you mean. But in this instance you are explaining talent through injustice, our grandmothers' gift through their condition as oppressed women – although there have been many great cooks who suffered neither from an inferiority of caste nor a life deprived of prestige or power. How do you reconcile this with your theory?'

'No chef can cook, nor has ever cooked, the way our grandmothers did. All the factors we have been evoking here' – and I place a slight emphasis on the 'we' to clearly point out that at this point I am the one who is officiating – 'have produced a very specific cuisine, that of women in their homes, within the enclosure of their private interior: a cuisine which sometimes might lack refinement, which always contains a "home-cooked" side to it, that is, solid and nourishing, made to "stick to your ribs" – but which is basically and above all intensely sensual: we understand that when we talk about "flesh" it is no mere coincidence that it evokes both the pleasures of the table and those of love. After all it was through their cooking that they lured, and seduced, and charmed – and that is what inspired it and made it like no other.'

Again he smiles at me. Then in front of all his crestfallen epigones – devastated because they fail to understand, *cannot* understand that despite performing their gastronomic balancing act, despite erecting temples to the glory of the goddess Grub, they have been upstaged by a wretched mongrel pup who came along with his gnawed yellow old bone in his sheepish muzzle, and who now sits here before them while they mourn – he says to me, 'So that we might quietly continue this fascinating discussion, would you do me the honour of joining me for lunch tomorrow at Lessière's?'

I called Anna some time ago and I understood that I would not be going. Not now. Not ever. This is the end of an epic tale, the story of my coming of age, which, as in the novels of the same description, went from wonder to ambition, from ambition to disillusion, and from disillusion to cynicism. The rather shy, sincere young man I once was has become a very influential critic – feared, respected, educated at the best university and welcomed in the best circles. But with each passing day and well ahead of time, he feels older and older, increasingly weary, increasingly useless: a clattering old fool, full of venom as he trots out the better part of a self which is inexorably crumbling away and portends nothing better than twilight years spent as a lucid, pitiful old bastard. And is that what he is feeling now? Is that what would steal secretly under his somewhat weary eyelids with a hint of sadness, a pinch of nostalgia? Shall I follow in his footsteps, experiencing the same regret, the same erring ways? Or am I just in a phase of feeling sorry for myself – since I am far, so far, from the brilliance of his private peregrinations? I shall never know.

The king is dead. Long live the king.

Fish

Rue de Grenelle, the Bedroom

Every summer we returned to Brittany. It was still the era when school did not start until mid-September; my grandparents, who had recently made their fortune, rented a large villa on the coast, at the end of the season, and the entire family would gather there. It was a miraculous time. I was not yet old enough to understand that these simple people, who had worked hard all their lives and upon whom fate had smiled somewhat late in life, had decided that, rather than keep their money, as others might have done, under their woollen mattress, they would spend it with their family and in their lifetime. I was, however, already aware that we children were being pampered, albeit in an intelligent way that still astonishes me, for I only ever spoiled my own children – spoiled in the strictest sense of the term. I caused them to rot and decompose, those three children who emerged from my wife's entrails, gifts I had negligently given to her in exchange for her decorative wifely abnegation – terrible gifts, when I think about it today, for what are children other than the monstrous excrescences of our own selves, pitiful substitutes for our unfulfilled desires? For the likes of me – people, in other words, who already have something which gives them pleasure in life – children are worthy of interest only when they finally leave home and become something other than one's own daughters or sons. I do not love them, I have never loved them, and I feel no remorse on that account. If they expend all their energy hating me with all their strength, that is no concern of mine; the only paternity that I might lay claim to is that of my own *oeuvre*. And the buried flavour that I cannot find is beginning to make me doubt even that.

As for my grandparents, they loved us in their way: undividedly. They had made their own children into an assortment of neuropaths and degenerates: a melancholy son, a hysterical daughter, another daughter who committed suicide, and finally my own father who escaped madness at the cost of all fantasy, and who chose a wife in his own image; what safeguarded my parents was the way they applied their apathy and mediocrity to protecting themselves from excess – from the abyss, in other words. And I was the only ray of sunshine in my mother's existence: I was her god, and a god I have remained; I have retained nothing of her sad face or her lifeless cooking or her somewhat plaintive voice, but I have preserved all her love, which endowed me with the self-assurance of a king. To have been adulated by one's mother . . . Thanks to her I have conquered empires, I have confronted life with an irresistible brutality which opened the gates of glory for me. The child who had everything has become a man without pity, thanks to the love of a shrew who, in the end, was resigned to gentleness solely by her lack of ambition.

With their grandchildren, on the other hand, my grandparents were the most charming of individuals. Deep in their souls they had a talent for the sort of good-natured and mischievous behaviour that had been restrained by their burden as parents, but as grandparents, they could give it free rein. The summer radiated freedom. Everything seemed possible in our world of fervid exploration, and of joyful, pretend secret outings on the rocks by the beach at nightfall; anything could happen, given the unprecedented generosity that extended invitations to all the neighbours at random on those summer days. My grandmother officiated at the stove with a haughty tranquillity. She weighed over fifteen stone, had a moustache, laughed like a man and barked at us with all the grace of a lorry driver whenever we ventured into the kitchen. Yet under the influence of her expert hands, the most banal substances were transformed into miracles of faith. White wine flowed freely and we ate and ate and ate. Sea urchins, oysters, mussels, grilled prawns, shellfish with mayonnaise, calamari in sauce, but also ('You can't change who you are!') daubes, blanquettes, paellas and poultry – roasted, stewed or à la crème; we were showered with food.

Once a month my grandfather would put on a strict and solemn expression at breakfast, then get up without a word and head off alone to the fish market. Then we knew that *the* day had come. My grandmother would raise her eyes to the heavens, mumble that 'as per usual the whole house will stink for ages', and mutter something rude about her husband's culinary talents. I personally felt moved to tears at the thought of what was to follow, and I may have known that she was joking, but I nevertheless fleetingly begrudged her the fact that she did not incline her head with humility at this sacred moment. An hour later my grandfather returned from the port with an enormous crate smelling of the sea. He sent us off to the beach – we were the 'brats', and we would head off all atremble with excitement, already home again in our thoughts but docile and mindful not to go against our grandfather's wishes. When we set off for home at one o'clock, after what was at best a distracted swim, so hopelessly did we anticipate the prospect of lunch, we could already catch a whiff of the heavenly smell from the corner of the street. I could have sobbed for joy.

The grilled sardines filled the entire neighbourhood with their ashy marine aroma. A thick grey smoke rose from the thujas that surrounded the garden. The men from the neighbouring houses came to lend my grandpa a hand. On enormous grills the little silvery fish were already turning crisp in the noon breeze.

35

There was laughter and talk, and bottles of well-chilled dry white wine were opened; the men sat down at last and the women came out of the kitchen with their piles of immaculate plates. My grandmother reached skilfully for a plump little fish, sniffed its perfume, and dropped it on the plate with a few others. With her big moist cow eyes she looked at me kindly and said, 'Here, littl'un, the first lot's for you! Goodness me, you just love 'em, don't you!' And everyone burst out laughing, and slapped me on the back while the prodigious sustenance was placed before me. I did not hear another thing. My eyes open wide, I stared at the object of my desire: the grey, blistered skin, with its long black stripes, that no longer even clung to the flesh it was covering. My knife slipped into the fish's spine and carefully divided the whitish meat: it was perfectly cooked, and came off in firm little strips without the least resistance.

In the flesh of grilled fish, from the humblest of mackerel to the most refined salmon, there is something that defies culture. Early man, in learning to cook fish, must have felt his humanity for the first time, in this substance where fire revealed both essential purity and wildness. To say that the flesh is delicate, that its taste is both subtle and expansive, that it stimulates the gums with a mixture of sharpness and sweetness; to say that the combination of the grilled skin's faint bitterness and the extreme smoothness of the firm, strong, harmonious flesh, filling one's mouth with a flavour from elsewhere, elevates the grilled sardine to the rank of culinary apotheosis, is at best like evoking the soporific virtues of opium. For what is at issue here is neither how delicate or sweet or strong or smooth the grilled sardine may be, but its wild nature. One must be strong in spirit to confront a taste like this; concealed within, very precisely, is the primitive brutality that forges our humanity when we come into contact with it. And one must be pure in spirit, as well, a spirit that knows how to chew with vigour, to the exclusion of any other food: I scorned the potatoes and salted butter which my grandmother had set out next to my plate, and relentlessly devoured the strips of fish.

Meat is virile, powerful; fish is strange and cruel. It comes from another world, a secret ocean that will never yield to us; it bears witness to the absolute relativity of our existence, and yet it offers itself to us through the ephemeral revelation of unknown realms. When I was savouring these grilled sardines, like an autistic child whom nothing could trouble at that point in time, I knew that this extraordinary confrontation with a sensation from elsewhere was making me human, bringing its contrasting nature to bear to teach me my human essence. Infinite, cruel, primitive, refined ocean: between our avid teeth we seize the products of your mysterious activity. The grilled sardine suffused my palate with its frank and exotic bouquet, with each mouthful I grew more mature, and every time my tongue caressed the marine ash of blistered skin I felt exalted.

But that is not what I have been looking for, either. I have brought to the surface of my memory forgotten sensations buried beneath the magnificence of my regal banquets; I have become reacquainted with the early stages of my vocation; I have exhumed the effluvia of my childhood soul. And that is not it. Time is pressing, and brings with it the uncertain yet terrifying contours of my ultimate failure. I do not want to give up. I am making an immoderate effort to remember. And what if, in the end, the thing that is taunting me is not even something delicious? Like Proust's abominable madeleine, that oddity of a pastry reduced one sinister and drab afternoon to a spoonful of spongy crumbs – supreme offence – in a cup of herbal tea, in actual fact my memory may merely be associated with some mediocre dish, and it is only the emotion attached to it that remains precious, and that might reveal to me a gift for living that I had not previously understood.

(Jean)

Café des Amis, 18th Arrondissement

Purulent old goatskin. Putrid rotting carcass. Die, just go ahead and die. Die in your silk sheets, in your pasha's bed, in your bourgeois cage, die, die, die. At least then we'll have your money, even if we'll never have your favour. All your big-shot foodie money can't do you an ounce of good any more, so it will go to other people, your rich landlord money, the cash from your corruption, your parasitical activities, all that food, all that luxury, such a waste . . . Die . . . Everyone is rushing to your side – Maman, Maman who really should leave you to die alone, abandon you the way you abandoned her, but she won't, she stays there, inconsolable, and she really believes she is losing everything. I'll never get it, why she's so blind, so resigned, and how she manages to convince herself that she has had the life she wanted, her vocation as a holy martyr; shit, it makes me want to puke, Maman, Maman . . . And then there's that dickhead Paul, behaving like the prodigal son, with his 'spiritual heir' hypocrisy, he must be crawling all over the bed, do you need a cushion, Uncle, would you like me to read you a few pages of Proust, or Dante, or Tolstoy? I can't stand him, that piece of crap, Mr Perfect Bourgeois with his distinguished gentlemanly airs, screwing the whores on Rue Saint-Denis; I've seen him, yes, I've seen him coming out of one of the buildings there . . . Oh, but what's the use, eh, what's the use of stirring all this up, stirring up my ugly-duckling bitterness, it will only prove the old man right: my children are imbeciles, that's what he used to say, quite calmly, in our presence, we were all embarrassed, except for him, of course, he couldn't even see how that might be *shocking*, not just saying it but even thinking it! My children are imbeciles, especially my son. He'll never amount to anything. No, you're wrong, Father, they have amounted to something, your brats, they are nothing more than your own creation, you chopped them up finely and spat them out and drowned them in a stinking gravy and that is what they have become: weaklings, losers, failures, sludge. And yet! And yet you could have made them gods, your kids. I remember how proud I used to feel when I went out with you, when you took me to a market or a restaurant; I was only little and you were so tall, with your big warm hand holding mine tightly, and your profile, when I saw it from below, the profile of an emperor, and your lion's mane! You had such a proud look and I was over the moon, over the moon to have a father like you . . . And now here I am, sobbing, my voice is breaking, my heart is broken, crushed; I hate you, I love you, and I hate my own ambivalence so much I could scream, fucking ambivalence that has ruined my life, because I am still your son, because I've never been anything other than the son of a monster!

The real ordeal is not leaving those you love but learning to live without those who don't love you. And my sorry life has been spent longing so ardently for all the love you have withheld, your absent love, oh for Christ's sake, is this the best I can do, weep over my miserable fate as a poor unloved little boy? There are far more important things, I'm going to die soon, too, and no one gives a damn, and I don't give a damn either, I don't give a damn because, right now, he is dying and I love the bastard, I love him, oh shit . . .

The Vegetable Garden

Rue de Grenelle, the Bedroom

My Aunt Marthe's house was a dilapidated old place buried in ivy, and because of its façade with one bricked-up window, there was something distinctly one-eyed about the place that perfectly suited both its surroundings and its occupant. Aunt Marthe, the eldest of my mother's sisters and the only one who did not inherit a nickname, was a sour, ugly, malodorous old maid who lived between her chicken coop and her rabbit hutches in unbelievable squalor. Indoors, as was to be expected, there was neither running water, electricity, telephone nor television. But above all, beyond this lack of creature comforts to which my love of country outings actually made me completely indifferent, we suffered at her place from the presence of a scourge that was far more dismaying: there was nothing in her house that was not sticky or did not cling to our fingers whenever we wanted to pick up a tool or our elbows had the misfortune to bump into a piece of furniture; even our eyes, literally, could perceive the viscous film that covered every single thing. We never lunched or dined with her there and, only too happy to plead the necessity for picnics ('The weather is so fine, it would be a crime not to have lunch on the banks of the Golotte'), we would head off elsewhere with relief in our hearts.

The countryside. All my life I have lived in the city, intoxicated with the marble surfaces that pave the vestibule of my residence, or the red carpet that muffles one's steps and feelings, or the Delft glass that decorates the stairwell, or the luxurious woodwork that discreetly panels the precious boudoir we call a lift. Every day, every week, when I returned from my meals in the provinces, I would find myself once again on the asphalt, and in the distinguished veneer of my bourgeois residence, locking up my hunger for greenery between four walls crammed full of masterpieces, and every time I would forget a little bit more that I was born to be among trees. The countryside . . . My green cathedral . . . It was there that my heart sang its most fervent hymns, that my eyes learned the secrets of looking, my taste buds the flavour of game and of the vegetable garden, and my nose the elegance of fragrances. For in spite of the repulsive aspect of her lair, Aunt Marthe did possess a treasure. I have met the greatest specialists in everything that has to do, however remotely, with the world of taste. Those who claim to be cooks must resort to all five senses to be truly cooks. A dish must delight the eye, the nose and the taste buds, of course – but also one's sense of touch, which directs the chef's choice on so many occasions and has its part to play in the celebration of fine food. It is true that hearing would seem to have no part to play, but one does not eat in silence, or in the midst of a din; any sound which interferes with the tasting process may either contribute or disturb that process, in such a way that a meal is indisputably kinaesthetic. Thus I was often called on to feast with specialists of smell who were lured by the aromas emanating from kitchens, after having been lured by those emanating from flowers.

Not one of them will ever have as fine a nose as Aunt Marthe. Because the old nag was a Nose, a true one, a great one, a huge Nose who didn't know she was a nose, but whose unprecedented sensitivity would never have suffered from competition, had there been any. Thus, this coarse, almost illiterate woman, this piece of human scum casting her rotten foul stench onto everyone around her, had created a garden fragrant with paradise. Through a knowing tangle of wild flowers, honeysuckle and old rose whose faded hue had been carefully preserved, a vegetable garden scattered with brilliant peonies and blue sage proudly displayed the most beautiful lettuce leaves in the region. Cascades of petunias, groves of lavender, a few steadfast box trees, ancestral wisteria along the front wall of the house: from this well-orchestrated jumble emanated the best of her being, that neither dirt nor fetid exhalations nor the sordid aspect of a life devoted to vacuousness could manage to enshroud. How many old women in the countryside are gifted in this way with an extraordinary sensory intuition which they apply to their gardening, or to making herbal potions, or to cooking rabbit stew with thyme, old women who then die as unknown geniuses, their gift ignored by all – for most often we fail to see that something so seemingly trivial and inconsequential, a chaotic garden deep in the countryside, can belong with the most beautiful works of art. In this reverie of flowers and vegetables, beneath my dust-brown feet I crushed the dry thick grass of the garden, and became drunk on its fragrances.

First of all, the geranium leaves: I would lie on my stomach among the tomatoes and peas and, swooning with pleasure, rub the leaves between my fingers: slightly acid, sufficiently tart with a vinegary insolence, but not so tart that they could fail to evoke at the same time the delicately bitter scent of candied lemon, with a hint of the acrid odour of tomato leaves, whose boldness and fruitiness they preserve – that is what geranium leaves exhale, that is what I grew drunk on, with my belly to the ground in the vegetable garden and my head in the flowers, ferreting for fragrance with all the concupiscence of the famished. Oh, magnificent memories of a time when I was the sovereign of a realm without artifice . . . In whole battalions, legions of red, white, yellow and pink carnations stood proudly in the four corners of the courtyard, swelling their ranks each year with new recruits to become an army of serried troops and, through some inexplicable miracle, they did not slump from the weight of their overgrown stems, but bravely lifted their odd, chiselled corollas, incongruous in such tight configuration, scowling, but wafting all around a powdery fragrance, like beauties on their way to the ball . . .

Above all there was the lime tree. Immense and decorative, from one year to the next it threatened to submerge the house with its tentacular foliage, which my aunt obstinately refused to prune: any discussion was out of the question. During the hottest days of summer, the tree's troublesome shade offered the most sweet-smelling of bowers. I would sit against the trunk on the little bench of worm-eaten wood and avidly inhale the scent of pure, velvety honey which came from the tree's pale-yellow flowers. A lime tree releasing its perfume at the end of the day is a rapture which leaves an indelible mark, and in the depths of our joy at being alive it traces a groove of happiness that the sweetness of a July evening alone cannot suffice to explain. Filling my lungs in memory, with that scent, which has not neared my nostrils in many a year, I have finally understood what it was that gave it its aroma: the complicity of honey and that very particular smell of the tree's leaves after a long spell of hot weather, when they are impregnated with the dust of the fine summer days, and this evokes the absurd yet sublime feeling of imbibing from the air a concentrated essence of summer. Oh those fine summer days! When your body is free of the constraints of winter, when at last you can feel the caress of a breeze against your naked skin, offered to the world, blatantly open to it, in an ecstasy of freedom regained . . . In the motionless air, saturated with the buzzing of invisible insects, time stands still . . . The poplar trees along the towpaths sing to the breezes a melody of verdant rustling, between light and shimmering shadow . . . A cathedral, yes, a cathedral of light-splattered greenery encircles me with its immediate, clear beauty . . . Even the jasmine at nightfall in the streets of Rabat never attained such evocative power . . . I am following the thread of a scent belonging to the lime . . . Languorous swaying of branches, a bee gathering pollen at the edge of my line of vision . . . I remember . . .

She had picked it, that particular one among all the others, she had not hesitated for an instant. I have since learned that this is what makes for excellence, this impression of ease and certainty in an instance where we know that it actually takes centuries of experience, a will of iron and the discipline of a monk. Where did Aunt Marthe derive her science from – a science made up of hydrometry, solar radiation, biological maturation, photosynthesis, geodesic orientations and many other factors that my ignorance will not venture to enumerate? For what an ordinary human might know from experience and reflection, she knew instinctively. Her acute discernment swept over the surface of the vegetable garden and measured its climate in a microsecond that no ordinary perception of time could detect – and she knew. She knew as surely and with the same nonchalance as if I had said, The weather is fine, she knew which of these little red globes had to be picked *now*. In her dirty hand, deformed by work in the fields, there it sat: crimson in its taut silken finery, undulating with the occasional more tender hollow, with a communicable cheerfulness about it like a plumpish woman in her party dress hoping to compensate for the inconvenience of her extra pounds by means of a disarming chubbiness that evokes an irresistible desire to bite into her flesh. Sprawled on the bench beneath the lime tree, lulled by the low murmuring of the leaves, I woke from a voluptuous nap, and beneath this canopy of sugary honey I bit into the fruit, I bit into the tomato.

In salads, baked, in ratatouille, in preserves, grilled, stuffed, cherry, candied, big and soft, green and acidic, honoured with olive oil or coarse salt or wine or sugar or hot pepper, crushed, peeled, in a sauce, in a stew, in a foam, even in a sorbet: I thought I had thoroughly covered the matter and, on more than one occasion, I wrote pieces inspired by the greatest chefs' menus claiming that I had penetrated its secret. What an idiot, what a pity . . . I invented mysteries where there were none, in order to justify my perfectly pathetic métier. What is writing, no matter how lavish the pieces, if it says nothing of the truth, cares little for the heart, and is merely subservient to the pleasure of showing one's brilliance? And yet I had always been acquainted with the tomato, since the time of Aunt Marthe's garden, since the summer when an ever more ardent sun kissed the timid little growths, since the moment my teeth tore into the flesh to splatter my tongue with the rich, warm and bountiful juice, whose essential generosity is masked by the chill of a refrigerator, or the affront of vinegar, or the false nobility of oil. Sugar, water, fruit, pulp, liquid or solid? The raw tomato, devoured in the garden when freshly picked, is a horn of abundance of simple sensations, a radiating rush in one's mouth that brings with it every pleasure. The resistance of the skin – slightly taut, just enough; the luscious yield of the tissues, their seed-filled liqueur oozing to the corners of one's lips, and that one wipes away without any fear of staining one's fingers; this plump little globe unleashing a flood of nature inside us: a tomato, an adventure.

Beneath the hundred-year-old lime, between perfume and palate, I would bite into the plump purple globes that Aunt Marthe had brought me with the vague sensation that I was in the presence of a capital truth. A capital truth – but one which, still, is not the one I seek now at the gates of death. It has been decreed that on this morning I shall drink my despair to the dregs, for I have strayed from the place to which my heart is calling. The raw tomato, no, that is not yet what I have been searching for . . . and now another raw delight has entered my thoughts.

(Violette)

Rue de Grenelle, the Kitchen

Poor Madame. To see her like this, in torment, she just doesn't know what to do any more. It's true he's in a very bad way . . . I didn't recognise him! I'd no idea how much a person could change in one day. Violette, said Madame, he's after some food or other, you understand, he's after something but he doesn't know what. At first I didn't understand. Some food. He's after some food, Madame, well, does he want it or not? He's searching, searching for something that would make him feel good, she answered, but he can't find it. And she was wringing her hands, what is he thinking, to get all worked up over some dish when you're about to die; if I were going to die tomorrow, you can be sure I wouldn't be bothered about eating!

I do everything here. Well, almost everything. When I first started here thirty years ago, it was as a cleaning lady. Madame and Monsieur had only just got married, they were not badly off, I think, but not wealthy either. There was just enough to hire a cleaning lady three times a week. The money came later, lots of money, I could see it was happening very quickly and that they expected there would be more and more money, because they moved into this big apartment, the same one we're in today, and Madame started doing a lot of work on the place, she was very cheerful, she was happy, you could tell, and she was so pretty! So once Monsieur was firmly established in his career they hired more staff and Madame kept me on as a 'housekeeper', with better pay, full time, to 'supervise' the others: the cleaning woman, the butler, the gardener (there's only a large terrace, but the gardener always finds things to do, in fact he's my husband, so there will always be a job for him). Mind now, don't go thinking there's no work for me to do. I run around all day, I have my inventories to draw up, lists, orders to give, and while I don't want to act all important, if I weren't here, frankly, nothing would run smoothly in this house.

I do like Monsieur. I know he's got his faults, and one of them is that he's made poor Madame so unhappy, not just today but right from the start, always off somewhere, always coming back and never asking for any news, looking at her as if she were transparent and giving her presents the way you give someone a tip. Not to mention the children. I wonder if Laura will come. I used to think, before, that when he got old everything would work out, that he'd end up being more gentle, and then grandchildren are supposed to reconcile parents with their children, it goes without saying. Of course, Laura doesn't have any children. But still. You'd think she'd come . . .

I like Monsieur for two reasons. First, because he has always been polite and kind to me, and to Bernard, my husband, as well. More polite and kinder than he is to his wife and kids. That's the way he is, well-mannered enough to say, 'Good morning, Violette, how are you today? Is your son feeling better?' but he hasn't said good morning to his wife for twenty years. The worst of it is that he seems sincere, with his big, loud, kindly voice, he's not proud, no, not at all, he's always very courteous to us. And he looks at me, and he pays attention to what I say to him, and he smiles because I'm always in a good mood, always busy doing something, I never rest and I know he's listening to my answers because he answers too when I question him in return: 'And you, sir, how are you this morning?' 'Fine, fine, Violette, but I'm behind with my work and it's not getting any better, I've got to get going,' and he winks at me before disappearing down the corridor. Now, he wouldn't be like that with his wife. He likes people like us, Monsieur does, he prefers us, you can tell. I think he feels more at ease with us than with all those upper-crust sorts he hangs around with: you can tell he's glad he can please them and impress them, stuff them full of food and watch them listening to him, but he doesn't like them; it's not his world.

The second reason I like Monsieur is kind of hard to put into words . . . it's because he farts in bed! The first time I heard it, I couldn't figure out what it was I'd heard, so to speak . . . And then it happened again, it was seven in the morning, it came from the corridor to the little drawing room where Monsieur sometimes slept when he came home late at night, a sort of detonation, a parp, but I mean really loud; I'd never heard anything like it! And then I understood, and I couldn't stop laughing, I laughed till I cried. I was bent over double, I had a bellyache, but at least I had the presence of mind to go to the kitchen, I sat down on the bench, I thought I'd never catch my breath! From that day on I've felt particularly well disposed towards Monsieur, yes, well disposed, because my husband farts in bed, too (but not as loud, all the same). A man who farts in bed, my grandmother used to say, is a man who loves life. And then, I don't know: it just made me feel closer to him . . .

I know exactly what it is that Monsieur wants. It's not a dish, it's not something to eat. It's the lovely blonde lady who came here twenty years ago with a sad look on her face, a very gentle lady, very elegant, who asked, 'Is Monsieur at home?' And I answered, 'No, but Madame is here.' She raised an eyebrow, I could tell she was surprised, and then she turned on her heel and I never saw her again, but I'm sure there was something between them and that if he didn't love his wife it was because he was missing the tall blonde lady in the fur coat.

Raw

Rue de Grenelle, the Bedroom

To return is to discover perfection. That is why only decadent civilisations are susceptible to the return: it is in Japan, where refinement has attained unequalled heights, at the heart of a millennial culture that has given humanity its greatest contributions, that the return to raw food, in its latest manifestation, has been possible. It is at the heart of old Europe – like my own self, endlessly dying – that for the first time since prehistory people have been eating raw meat seasoned with a mere sprinkling of spices.

Raw food. One would be wrong to believe that this involves nothing more than the coarse consumption of unprepared matter! Slicing into raw fish is like cutting into stone. To a novice a block of marble seems monolithic. If you try to place your chisel at random and strike a blow, the tool will jump out of your hands, while the stone will preserve its integrity, unaffected. A good marble-worker knows his material. He senses where the cut – which already exists, just waiting to be revealed – will yield to his blow, and he has already divined, to the nearest millimetre, the shape that will emerge, a figure which only the uninformed might impute to the will of the sculptor. No, on the contrary, the sculptor merely unveils the shape – for talent consists not in inventing shapes but in causing those that were invisible to emerge.

The Japanese chefs of my acquaintance only became masters in the art of raw fish after years of apprenticeship, during which the cartography of flesh was gradually brought to light. It is true that some people already have the gift, can feel beneath their fingers the fault lines along which the offered creature shall be transformed into delectable sashimi, of the sort only experts know how to exhume from the tasteless entrails of the fish. But they do not become artists for all that until they have mastered their innate talent, and learned that instinct alone cannot suffice: they will also need agility in slicing, discernment in determining what is best, and strength of character to reject anything that is mediocre. The chef Tsuno, the greatest of them all, was known to take from a gigantic salmon only a single tiny piece that seemed quite derisory. In this matter, in fact, abundance is meaningless: perfection orders everything. A tiny fragment of fresh flesh, on its own, naked, raw: perfect.

I knew him when he was already advanced in years, when he had deserted his own kitchen and would observe the customers from behind the bar, without ever touching a plate. Once in a great while, however, in honour of a guest or a particular occasion, he would return to his work – but only for sashimi. In his later years these already exceptional occasions became increasingly rare, until they came to be considered extraordinary events.

I was a young critic at the time, whose career was still a matter of promising beginnings, and I still concealed the arrogance that only later would be recognised as the mark of my genius, but which, at the time, would have come across as mere pretension. It was therefore with feigned humility that I went to sit at the Kamogawa sushi bar, alone, for a dinner that I expected to be honourable. I had never tasted raw fish in my life, and hoped to discover a new source of pleasure. Nothing in my budding career as a gastronome had in fact prepared me for such a thing. The only word that mattered to me at the time was *terroir* – but today I know that a *terroir* only exists by virtue of one's childhood mythology, and that if we have invented these worlds of tradition rooted deep in the land and identity of a region, it is because we want to solidify and objectify the magical bygone years that preceded the horror of becoming an adult. Only a fanatical will to make a vanished world endure despite the passing of time can explain this belief in the existence of a *terroir* – an entire world that has disappeared, a mixture of flavours, smells, scattered fragrances that has left its sediment in ancestral rites and local dishes, crucibles of illusory memories that seek to make gold from sand, eternity from time. On the contrary, there is no great cuisine without evolution, without erosion and forgetting. Invention must constantly be invoked upon the countertop, and past and future, here and elsewhere, raw and cooked, savoury and sweet shall all be mixed, for it is this inventiveness that has turned cookery into an art that thrives untrammelled by the obsession of those who do not wish to die.

It is no exaggeration therefore to say that between cassoulets and cabbage stew I arrived at the Kamogawa sushi bar completely innocent of any contact with – but not of preconceived ideas of – Japanese cuisine. Hidden by a host of cooks, at the back to the right, was a little man slumped in a chair. The restaurant was bare, with its spartan room and basic chairs, but a cheerful hubbub reigned, the sort you hear in places where guests are satisfied with the food and with the service. Nothing surprising. Nothing special. Why did he do it? Did he know who I was, had word of my budding reputation in the little gastronomic fraternity reached the ears of this blasé old man? Was it for his sake? Was it for mine? What causes a mature man, who has outlived all his emotions, to revive a faltering internal flame after all, and for one last show set his vital force ablaze? What is at stake in the confrontation between a man who is abdicating and one who is conquering – is it lineage, is it renunciation? It remains a fathomless mystery: not once did he turn his gaze on me, except at the end – his eyes empty, ravaged, signifying nothing.

When he got up from his rickety chair, a stony silence gradually fell over the restaurant. First of all upon the cooks, who were in a petrified stupor, and then, it was as if an invisible wave suddenly broke over all those present, upon the customers at the bar, then those in the dining area, until the silence reached those who had just come in and who stood watching the scene, dumbfounded. He had got up without a word and walked over to the counter, opposite me. The man whom earlier I had assumed was leading the team bowed briefly, a gesture filled with the absolute respect so characteristic of Asian cultures, and then he slowly stepped back, with all the others, towards the gaping kitchens, although they did not go in, but just stood there, motionless, devout. Chef Tsuno elaborated his composition there before me with gentle, sparing gestures, displaying an economy of movement that bordered on indigence, but I could see beneath his palm the birth and blossoming, in mother-of-pearl and moiré, of slivers of flesh, pink and white and grey; fascinated, I sat watching the miracle.

It was dazzling. What would then pass through the barrier of my teeth was neither matter nor water, merely an intermediary substance that had retained of the former the texture and consistency that prevented it from evaporating into nothingness, and had borrowed from the latter its miraculous fluidity and smoothness. True sashimi is not so much bitten into as allowed to melt on the tongue. It calls for slow, supple chewing, not to bring about a change in the nature of the food, but merely to allow one to savour its airy, satiny texture. Yes, it is like a fabric: sashimi is velvet dust, verging on silk, or a bit of both, and the extraordinary alchemy of its gossamer essence allows it to preserve a milky density unknown even by clouds. The first pink mouthful to evoke such a thrill was salmon, but I had yet to try plaice, scallop and octopus. Salmon is oily and sweet, despite its essential leanness; octopus is pure and rigorous, loath to divulge its secret liaisons to one's bite, and then only after a long resistance. I stared at the strange, lacy little piece of flesh before seizing upon it, all marbled pink and purple but almost black at the tip of its crenellated excrescences, clumsily picked it up with my chopsticks, which only complied with difficulty, placed it upon my tongue – which contracted at such novel density – and shivered with pleasure. Between the two, between the salmon and the octopus, came the entire palette of sensations, each characterised by the same compact fluidity which places heaven on one's tongue and makes any additional liquid, whether it is water, Kirin or warm saké, utterly superfluous. As for the scallop, it was so light and evanescent that it slipped away the moment it arrived, but long after, my cheeks recalled the effects of its profound caress. Last of all came the plaice, which, mistakenly, seemed to be the most rustic of all, for it is a lemony delicacy, and its exceptional constitution is confirmed the moment one bites into it and discovers its stupefying plenitude.

That is sashimi: a fragment of the cosmos within reach of one's heart, but, alas, light years from the fragrance or taste that is fleeing my wisdom, or is it my inhumanity . . . I thought that by evoking this subtle adventure into the territory of raw delights, a thousand leagues from the barbarity of those who devour animals, something might give off the perfume of authenticity that is inspiring that unknown memory, the memory I despair of ever capturing . . . Shellfish, yet again, it must be shellfish: perhaps it's simply not the right one?

(Chabrot)

Rue de Bourgogne, Consulting Room

Three possible paths.

The asymptotic path: a wretched salary, green over-alls, long shifts as a houseman, a probable career, the path of power, the path of honours. Professor of Cardiology. The health-service hospital, devotion to the cause, love of science: just the right amount of ambition, nous and skill. I was ripe for all that.

The middle path: everyday life. Lots and lots of money. A posh clientele, teeming with depressive bourgeois ladies, rich and extravagant old men, gilded young drug addicts, angina, flu and long and immeasurable ennui. The Montblanc my wife presents me with every 25th of December slides over the white-ness of the prescription pad. I raise my head, crack a smile at the right moment, a bit of comfort here, a bit of politeness there, a lot of false humanity everywhere and for a price I am able to grant Madame Derville, the wife of the Chairman of the Bar, absolution from the anxieties caused by her condition as an incurable hysteric.

The tangential path: treat souls not bodies. Journalist, writer, painter, *éminence grise*, a mandarin of letters, archaeologist? Anything at all, save the panels of my worldly doctor's surgery, save the famous and well-paid anonymity of my curative charge, in my affluent neighbourhood, in my minister's armchair . . .

The middle path, naturally. And stretching ahead, decades of nagging dissatisfaction, inner turmoil, sometimes eating away at me, sometimes virulent, sometimes hidden – but always present.

The first time he consulted me, I caught a glimpse of my salvation. He made a gift to me of the very thing that I – too corrupted by my bourgeois blood to renounce it – could not be, merely by tacitly agreeing to be my client, simply by frequenting my waiting room on a regular basis, with his ordinary docile manner of a patient who makes no fuss. Later he gave me another gift, magnanimously: that of his conversation. Worlds hitherto unknown to me suddenly appeared, and the very thing that my flame had always coveted so ardently, and had despaired of ever obtaining, was suddenly mine, thanks to him, vicariously.

To live vicariously: to give birth to one chef and be another's gravedigger, to extract words from a feast, phrases, symphonies of language, and to bring forth the dazzling beauty inherent in a meal; to be a Maître, a Guide, a Divinity; to touch inaccessible spheres with one's mind, to penetrate stealthily into the labyrinths of inspiration, come close to perfection, and touch on Genius! What should one's preference be, truly? To live one's sorry little life as a good obedient *Homo sapiens*, without purpose, without salt, because one is too weak to stick to one's objective? Or, almost trespassing, to share endlessly in the ecstasy of another who knows his quest, who has already begun his crusade and who, because he has an ultimate goal, partakes of immortality?

Later still, there came other generous gifts: his friendship. By accepting the gaze he bestowed upon me, in the privacy of our man-to-man conversations where I became, in the heat of my passion for Art, the witness, the disciple, the protector and admirer all at the same time, I received a hundredfold the fruit of my willing subordination. His friendship! Who has not dreamt of friendship with a Great Man of our century, who has not longed to be on familiar terms with the Hero, to embrace the prodigal son, the great Maître of those who love to gorge themselves on fine fare? His friend! His friend and

55

confidant, granted the ultimate privilege, oh how precious and painful at the same time, to have to bring him the news of his own death . . . Tomorrow? At dawn? Or during the night? The night . . . It is my night too, because the witness dies when he can no longer testify, because the disciple dies in the agony of loss, because the protector dies when he has failed, and the admirer, finally, dies from adoring a corpse doomed to the tranquillity of the graveyard . . . My night . . . But I regret nothing, and ask for everything: because it was he, because it was myself.

The Mirror

Rue de Grenelle, the Bedroom

His name was Jacques Destrères. It was at the very
beginning of my career. I had just completed an
article on the speciality of the Gerson restaurant, the
very article that would revolutionise the accepted structure of
my profession and place me in the firmament of food criticism.
I awaited with excitement yet confidence what was to follow,
and had taken refuge with my uncle, my father's older brother,
an old bachelor who knew how to live and whom everyone in
my family regarded as an eccentric. He had never married, nor
had we ever even seen a woman by his side, and my father
suspected him of being 'one of those'. He had done well in
business and in his mature years had retired to a lovely little
property near the Rambouillet forest, where he spent tranquil
days pruning his rose bushes, walking his dogs, smoking a
cigar in the company of a few old business associates and
concocting his little bachelor's meals.

Sitting in his kitchen, I watched him at work. It was
wintertime. I had had an early lunch at Groers, in Versailles,
and then made my way along the snowy little back roads in
what was an exceedingly good mood. The fire was burning
merrily in the hearth, and my uncle was preparing a meal. The
kitchen at my grandmother's had accustomed me to a noisy,
feverish atmosphere where, amidst the clanging of saucepans,
the sizzling of butter and the chop-chop of knives, toiled a
virago in a trance, and only her long experience granted her an
aura of serenity – of the sort displayed by martyrs in the flames

57

of hell. Jacques, on the other hand, undertook everything with moderation. He did not hurry, nor was he slow. Every movement came in its own good time.

He rinsed the jasmine rice in a silvery little colander, drained it, poured it into a saucepan, covered it with one and a half times its volume in salted water, put a lid on the pan, and let it cook. The prawns waited in an earthenware bowl. While he chatted to me, mostly about my article and my plans, he shelled the prawns with painstaking concentration. Not for one moment did he step up the pace, not for one moment did he slow down. When the last little arabesque had been stripped of its protective shell, he conscientiously washed his hands with a soap that smelled of milk. With the same serene uniformity in his movements, he placed a cast-iron griddle pan on the stove, poured a trickle of olive oil into it, let it heat up, then scattered the peeled prawns into the pan. His wooden spatula adroitly circled the shellfish, not allowing a single tiny crescent to escape, scooping them from every side and causing them to dance on the fragrant pan. Then some curry powder. Neither too much nor too little. A sensual dust tinged the pinky copper of the crustaceans with an exotic gold: the Orient, reinvented. Salt, pepper. With his scissors he snipped a sprig of coriander over the frying pan. Finally, very quickly, a capful of cognac, a match; a long, angry flame leapt up from the pan, like a shout or a cry set free at last, a raging sigh fading as quickly as it flared.

Waiting patiently on the marble table were a porcelain plate, a crystal glass, superb cutlery and an embroidered linen napkin. On the plate he carefully arranged, with the wooden spoon, half of the prawns, and the rice, which had been placed in a tiny bowl then turned upside down to create a plump little dome, crowned with a mint leaf. Into the glass he poured himself a generous helping of a transparent wheat-coloured liquid.

'Shall I pour you a glass of Sancerre?'

I shook my head. He sat down at the table.

A bite to eat. This is what Jacques Destrères called a bite to eat. And I knew he wasn't joking, that every day he would take great pains to cook himself a little mouthful of paradise, unaware of how refined his everyday fare was, a true gourmet; he lived every day as an authentic aesthete, where absolutely nothing was staged. Without touching the food he had prepared before my eyes, I watched him eat with the same detached, subtle care that he had put into cooking his meal, and this meal that I did not touch remained one of the most delicious I have ever tasted in my life.

Tasting is an act of pleasure, and writing about that pleasure is an artistic gesture, but the only true work of art, in the end, is another person's feast. Jacques Destrères's meal had all the perfection of a feast because it was not my feast, because it did not spill over into the before and after of my everyday life, and it could remain in my memory as a closed and self-sufficient unity, a unique moment etched there outside time and space, a pearl of my spirit released from the feelings in my life. As if one were looking at a room reflected in a sunburst mirror, which turns into a picture because it is no longer opened onto something else, but suggests an entire world without an elsewhere, strictly confined within the edges of the mirror and isolated from any life around it, so another person's meal is enclosed within the frame of our gaze, and is exempt from the infinite vanishing line of our own memories or plans. I would have liked to live that life, the one evoked by the mirror, or by Jacques's plate; a life without prospects, for with them the possibility of that life becoming a work of art would vanish; a life with neither once upon a time, nor ever after, with neither surroundings nor horizons: just the here and now – beautiful, full, enclosed.

*

But that is not it. Everything that fine restaurants brought to my nourishing genius, everything that Destrères's prawns might have suggested to my intelligence cannot teach my heart a thing. Spleen. Black sun.

The sun . . .

(Gégène)

Corner of Rue de Grenelle and Rue du Bac

We're cut from the same cloth, you and me.

There are two kinds of passers-by. First of all, the most common kind, even though it does contain some nuances: these are the people who won't ever meet my gaze, or if they do, it is just fleetingly, when they give me some change. There's a faint smile there too, sometimes, but always slight embarrassment, and then they hurry away fast as they can. Or they don't stop at all and go by as quickly as possible, with their guilty conscience bothering them for a hundred yards or so – fifty before, when they've seen me from a distance and make haste to screw their head in the other direction, until they're safely fifty yards past the down-and-out, when their head can regain its customary mobility – then they can forget me, they can breathe easy again, and that wrenching moment of pity and shame gradually fades away. I know what those people say when they go home at night, if they even think about it again, in some place deep in their unconscious: 'It's awful, there are more and more of them, it breaks your heart, I give them something, of course I do, but after the second one I have to draw the line, I know, it's arbitrary, it's horrible, but you can't go on giving endlessly, when I think of all the taxes we pay, it shouldn't be up to us to give, it's the State which is at fault, it's the State which isn't doing its bit, and even so it's a good job we've got a left-wing government, otherwise it would be even worse. So, what's

61

for dinner tonight, pasta?'

They're fucking scum, that lot. And that's being polite. To hell with them, those pinky bourgeois, they want to have their cake and eat it, they want their season ticket to the Châtelet and to see the have-nots rescued from poverty, they want their tea at Mariage's and all men on earth to be equal, they want their holiday in Tuscany and to see the pavements swept clean of anything that might stimulate their guilt, they want to pay their cleaning lady with cash and they want you to listen to their altruistic I'm-a-defender-of-humanity tirades. The State, the State! They're like illiterate folk who adore the king and accuse only the evil corrupt ministers of all the ills they're subject to; it's the Godfather saying to his minions, 'I don't like the look of this guy,' without acknowledging that what he has just ordered in a veiled sort of way is the man's execution; it's the bullied sons or daughters who insult the social worker asking for explanations from unworthy parents! The State! It's only fair to go after the State when you want to blame someone else, even if that someone else is none other than your own self!

And then there's the other kind. The brutes, the real bastards, the ones who don't hurry by, don't look away, they look right at me with their cold gaze, not a drop of compassion; tough luck, you old tramp, you can just snuff it if you couldn't work out how to get on in life, no indulgence for riffraff or the plebs vegetating in their subhuman cardboard boxes, we'll give them no quarter, it's win or lose, and if you think I'm ashamed of my money, well, you're mistaken.

For ten years, day after day, he would set out from his palace and deliberately walk right by me with his smug rich man's step, and he'd stare down my plea with a calm and scornful gaze.

If I were him, I'd do the same. People shouldn't think that all tramps are lefties and that poverty makes you a revolutionary. And since word has it he's going to die, I say to him, 'Go ahead and die, mate, die from all the money you never gave me, die from all your rich-bastard banquets, die from your life of power, but I sure won't be throwing up a cheer. We're cut from the same cloth, you and me.'

Bread

Rue de Grenelle, the Bedroom

We were breathless; it was time to leave the beach. The day had already seemed both deliciously short and long. The shoreline at this point, a long sandy arc stretching lazily into the distance and devoured by waves, offered us the most heedless of swims, with the maximum of pleasure and the minimum risk. Since morning, with my cousins, we had been diving over and over into the breakers, or taking flight from their crests, breathless, inebriated from the endless rollers, only returning to the common assembly point – the family parasol – just long enough to gobble a fritter or a bunch of grapes before racing hell for leather back into the ocean. There were times, however, when I would drop flat onto the hot, crunching sand and find myself instantly transfixed by a daze of well-being, only barely conscious of the drowsiness in my body and the customary sounds of the beach – from the cry of gulls to the laughter of children – an interlude of intimacy in the very singular stupor of happiness. But most of the time I drifted with the waves, surfacing and disappearing beneath their liquid, moving mass. Childhood exaltation: how many years do we spend forgetting the passion we breathed into any activity that held a promise of pleasure? Why are we now so rarely capable of such total commitment, such elation, such flights of charming lyricism? There was so much exultation about those days spent swimming, so much simplicity . . . so soon replaced, alas, by the ever-increasing difficulty in finding pleasure in things . . .

At around one in the afternoon we would strike camp. On our way back to Rabat, a dozen or so miles away, in the furnace that was the car, I could admire the waterfront at my leisure. I never tired of it. Later, as a young man who no longer partook of those Moroccan summers, I would occasionally conjure up the tiniest details of the road leading from the beach at Sables d'Or to the town, and in town I would go back over the streets and gardens with painstaking euphoria. It was a lovely road that overlooked the Atlantic in many spots; villas submerged in oleander offered glimpses through the false transparency of wrought iron onto the sunny life being lived behind those gates; further along was the ochre fortress over-looking the emerald water, and only much later would I learn that it was a grisly prison; then there was the little beach of Temara, sheltered, protected from wind and current, and I eyed it scornfully with the disdain of those who only appre-ciate the sea for its harshness and turbulence; the next beach along, too dangerous for swimming, had a scattering of intrepid fishermen, their brown legs whipped by waves as if the ocean wanted to swallow them in a raging roar; then came the outskirts of the city, the souk teeming with sheep and the light-coloured canvas of awnings snapping in the wind, the neighbourhoods swarming with joyful, noisy people, poor but healthy in the salt air. The sand clung to my ankles, my cheeks were burning, I grew drowsy with the heat in the car and let myself be lulled by the melodic yet forceful tones of Arabic, rocked to the rhythm of incomprehensible snatches of conversation stolen through the open window. A sweet ordeal, the sweetest of all: those who have spent their summers by the seaside know what this means, the exasperating necessity of *heading back*, of leaving the water for the land, of enduring the discomfort of becoming heavy and sweaty once again; they will know what it means, they have cursed it, but remember it, on other occasions, as a blessed moment. The holiday rituals, immutable sensations: the taste of salt at the corner of one's lips, shrivelled fingertips, hot, dry skin, sticky hair still dripping slightly down one's neck, shortness of breath, what a pleasure it was, how easy it was . . . Once we arrived home we would make a dash for the shower and re-emerge gleaming, our skin soft, our hair tamed, and the afternoon would begin with a meal.

We would buy it carefully wrapped in newspaper, at a little shop outside the city walls before we climbed back into the car.. I would look at it out of the corner of my eye; I was still too dazed to make the most of its presence, but I was reassured to know it was there, for 'afterwards', for 'lunch'. Strange . . . That this most visceral memory of bread, emerging on this day of death, should be that of a Moroccan *kesra*, a lovely, flat round, closer to a cake in consistency than to a baguette, does not fail to leave me pondering. Whatever the case may be, once I was rinsed off and dressed, blissfully awaiting my post-beach stroll through the medina, I would sit down at the table, tear off a first conquering mouthful from the sizeable chunk that my mother handed me, and in the yielding, golden warmth of this food I found once again the consistency of sand, its colour and welcoming presence. Bread, beach: two related sources of warmth, two alluring accomplices; every time, an entire world of rustic joy invades our perception. It's a fallacy to claim that the nobility of bread lies in the way it suffices unto itself while accompanying all other dishes. If bread 'suffices unto itself', it is because it is multiple, not because it exists in multiple variants but in its very essence: bread is rich, bread is diverse, bread is a microcosm. In bread one can find dazzling variety, akin to a miniature world, which reveals its inner workings as it is consumed. You storm it through an initial encounter with the barrier of crust, then yield to wonder the moment you are through, as the fresh soft interior consents.

There is such a divide between the crunchy shell – on occasion as hard as stone, at other times mere show, quickly yielding to the charge – and the tenderness of the inner substance, which lodges in one's cheeks with a docile charm, that one is almost at a loss. The fissures in the envelope are like surreptitious reminders of the countryside: one thinks of a ploughed field, of a peasant in the evening air; the village steeple has just rung seven o'clock; the peasant is wiping his forehead with the lapel of his jacket, his labours done.

Where the crust meets the soft bread, on the other hand, our inner gaze encounters a mill; the dust from the wheat whirls around the millstone, the air is infested with a volatile powder; and the picture changes once again, because your palate has just taken possession of the honeycombed foam, now freed from its yoke, and the labour of the jaw can begin. It is indeed bread, and yet you can eat it like cake; but chewing bread, unlike pastry, or even sweet breakfast rolls, leads to a surprising result, to a . . . sticky result. As you chew and chew upon the soft interior, a sticky mass is formed, which no air can penetrate: the bread adheres – yes, like glue. If you have never dared to take a mass of soft dough between your teeth and tongue and palate and cheeks, you have never thrilled to the feeling of jubilant ardour that viscosity can convey. It is no longer bread, nor dough, nor cake that we are masticating; it is something like our own self, what our own secret tissues must taste like, as we knead them with our expert mouths, saliva and yeast mingling in ambiguous fraternity.

Around the table, we ruminated in silence, conscientiously. There do exist some strange communions, after all . . . We were far from the rituals and banquets of institutional ceremonies – it was not a religious act of breaking bread and rendering grace to heaven, yet we were nevertheless united in a holy communion that caused us to attain, unbeknownst to us, a higher, all-decisive truth. And while a few of us might have been vaguely aware of this mystical orison, misguidedly attributing it to the pleasure of being together, of sharing a consecrated delicacy, within the convivial and relaxed atmosphere of summer holidays, I knew that their misapprehension arose for lack of the words and knowledge with which to express and illuminate such an exalted moment. The rural countryside, far from town; the gentle way of life and organic elasticity: there is all that in bread, whether the bread is from here or elsewhere. That is what, without the shadow of a doubt, makes bread the preferred vehicle for inner contemplation, for drifting in search of ourselves.

After this initial appetising contact, I would prepare for the next round of hostilities. Fresh salad – no need to point out the degree to which carrots and potatoes cut into tiny regular dice and seasoned with a hint of coriander are an improvement upon their more coarsely chopped fellows; then a bounty of tagines, causing me to lick my chops and stuff my face like an angel, without remorse or regret. But my mouth had not forgotten, my mouth remembered that this festive meal had been inaugurated by the encounter between its mandibles and a tender doughy mouthful, and even though to prove my gratitude I would go on to swoop the morsel into my plate to mop up all the sauce, I knew my heart was no longer in it. With bread, as with everything, it is the first time that counts.

I recall the flowery luxuriance of the Oudaia tea room, whence we could look out onto Salé and the sea, in the distance, just below the river which flowed beneath the city walls; the colourful narrow streets of the medina; the jasmine cascading down the walls of the inner courtyards, a poor man's wealth a thousand leagues from the luxury of perfumers in the West; life under the sun, in the end, which is not the same as life elsewhere, because living outdoors one views space differently . . . and the bread, round and flat, a dazzling aubade to the union of the flesh. I can tell . . . I can tell that I am close. There is something of all this in the thing I am searching for. There is something . . . but that's not quite it . . . bread . . . bread . . . But what else could it be? What else do men on earth live by, if not bread?

(Lotte)

Rue Delbet

I always said, I don't want to go there, I like Granny but I don't like Grandpa, he frightens me, he has big black eyes, and he's never happy to see us, never happy at all. That's why it's weird today. Because for once I would like to go there, I'd like to see Granny, and then Rick, and Maman is the one who doesn't want to go, she says Grandpa is sick and we're going to disturb him. Grandpa sick? It can't be. Jean is sick, yes, he's very sick but that doesn't matter, I like to be with him, I like it in summer when we go to the pebbly beach together, he takes a pebble and then he looks at it and he makes up a story, if it's a big fat one it's a man who's eaten too much, so now he can't walk any more, he rolls, and rolls, or else it's a little flat one, he's been walked on and boom, flat as a pancake, and lots of other stories like that.

As for Grandpa, he never told me any stories, never, he doesn't like stories, and he doesn't like children, and he doesn't like noise, I remember one day, at Rudegrenele I was playing nicely with Rick and then with Anaïs, Paul's sister's daughter, we were having a good laugh, and he turned and looked at us, a nasty look, a *really* nasty look, I felt like crying and hiding, I didn't feel like laughing any more at all, and he said to Granny but he didn't even look at her, 'This noise must stop.' So Granny put on her sad expression, she didn't answer him, she came to talk to us and she said, 'Come, children, let's go and play out on the square, Grandpa is tired.' When we got back from the square Grandpa had left and we didn't see him any more, we had dinner with Granny and Maman, and Adèle, Paul's sister, and we had a really good time again but I could see that Granny was sad.

When I ask Maman questions she always answers, No, everything is fine, all that is grown-ups' business, I mustn't worry about all that and she loves me very very much. That I know. But I also know a lot of other things. I know that Grandpa doesn't love Granny any more, and that Granny doesn't love herself any more, that Granny loves Jean more than Maman or Laura but Jean hates Grandpa and Grandpa thinks Jean's disgusting. I know that Grandpa thinks my papa is an idiot. I know that Papa is cross with Maman for being Grandpa's daughter, but also because she wanted to have me, and he didn't want any children, or at least not yet; I also know that Papa loves me very much and maybe even that he's mad at Maman for loving me so much when he didn't want me at all, and I know Maman is cross with me a little sometimes because she wanted me when Papa didn't. Oh yes, I know all that. I know that they're all unhappy because nobody loves the right person the way they should and because they don't understand that it's really their own self that they're cross with.

People think that children don't know anything. It's enough to make you wonder if grown-ups were ever children themselves once.

The Farm

Rue de Grenelle, the Bedroom

I eventually ended up at this spruce little farm on the Côte de Nacre after two hours of fruitless efforts to find an auberge that had just recently opened and which, I'd been told, was somewhere near Colleville and the American cemetery. I have always liked this part of Normandy. Not for its cider, or its apples, its cream or its *poulets flambés au calvados* but for its vast beaches, where the strand is laid bare by the low tide, and where I truly grasped the meaning of the expression 'between heaven and earth'. I took long walks along Omaha Beach, I was somewhat stunned by solitude and space, I watched the gulls and the dogs roaming in the sand, I raised my palm to shelter my eyes to study the horizon, which taught me nothing, and I felt content and trusting, reinvigorated by this silent escapade.

That morning, a fine summer morning, clear and cool, I had been wandering in search of my auberge with increasing bad humour, lost down unlikely sunken lanes, gleaning along the way only contradictory directions. I eventually set off down a little road that ended in a cul-de-sac in the yard of a Norman stone farmhouse with a porch crowned by an impressive wisteria, windows overwhelmed by red geraniums, and freshly painted white shutters. At the front of the house, in the shade of a lime tree, a table had been set and five people (four men and a woman) were finishing their lunch. They did not know the address of the place I was looking for. When I enquired, for lack of a better solution, whether there was somewhere not too far away where I could find something to eat, they sniffed with a hint of scorn. 'Better off eating at home,' said one of the men in a tone that was heavy with innuendo. The man I assumed to be the master of the house placed his hand on the roof of my car, leant in towards me, and suggested without further ado that I share their luncheon with them. I accepted.

Sitting beneath the lime tree, which was so fragrant that I nearly lost my appetite, I listened to them conversing over their coffee and calvados while the farmer's wife, a plump young woman with a winsome dimple on either side of the corners of her mouth, served me with a smile.

Four *fine de claire* oysters, cold and salty, with neither lemon nor seasoning. Swallowed slowly, blessed for the imperious chill with which they cloaked my palate. 'Oh, this is all that is left, there was a gross, twelve dozen, but the men, when they come in from work, have an appetite.' She laughed softly.

Four oysters, unembellished. A complete and uncompromising prelude, royal in unpolished modesty. A glass of dry white wine, chilled, with a fruity refinement – 'it's a Saché, we have a cousin in Touraine who gives us a good price!'

This is just to work up an appetite. The men next to me are unbelievably garrulous, talking cars. Cars that run. Cars that don't. Then there are those that grumble, or rebel, or make a fuss, or backfire, or chug breathlessly, or have trouble going up the hills, or skid in the turns, the ones that judder, or smoke, or hiccup, or cough, or nose up, or strike back. Memories of a particularly stubborn Simca 1100 are honoured with a long tirade. A nasty cold-arsed bitch of a car that wouldn't start even in the middle of summer. They all nod their heads, indignantly.

Two thin slices of raw smoked ham, silky and supple along languid folds, some salted butter, a hunk of bread. An overdose of vigorous taste and smooth texture: improbable but delectable. Another glass of the same white wine, which will accompany me for the rest of the meal. An enticing, charming, beguiling prologue.

'Yes, the forest is full of it' is the reply to my polite question about game in the region. 'In fact,' says Serge (there is also Claude and Christian, the master of the house, but I can't recall the name of the other fellow), 'it's often the cause of accidents.'

A few green asparagus stems, plump and tender enough to make you swoon. 'This will keep you going while the rest is reheating,' says the young woman hastily, no doubt thinking that I am surprised to see such a meagre main course. 'No, no,' I said, 'it's magnificent.' Exquisite tone, rural, almost bucolic. She blushes and hurries away with a laugh.

Next to me, the conversation continues in finer form than ever, about game animals unexpectedly crossing the road through the forest. There is talk of a certain Germain who, on a moonless night, ran over an adventurous wild boar and, thinking in the dark that it was dead, tossed it into his boot ('Just think, what luck!'), set off on his way. Meanwhile the beast gradually came to and started to kick about in the boot ('What a racket!') and then, by dint of so much thumping with its muzzle, dented the car and managed to escape into the night. They laugh like children.

'Leftovers' (enough to feed a regiment) of fattened chicken. An overabundance of cream, chunks of bacon, a pinch of black pepper, potatoes which I suspect come from Noirmoutier – and not an ounce of fat.

The conversation has taken a detour, setting off down the sinuous winding road of local spirits. Good ones, not so good ones, and those that are frankly undrinkable; illicit liquors, ciders that are too fermented, with rotten apples that were

74

poorly washed and poorly crushed and poorly picked; supermarket calvados that tastes like syrup, and then the true calvados, which scorches your throat but perfumes your palate. The liquor of a certain renowned Père Joseph sets everyone off in peals of laughter: a disinfectant, that much is for sure, but not a *digestif*!

'I'm so sorry,' says the young woman, who does not speak with the same accent as her husband, 'there's no more cheese, I have to go shopping this afternoon.'

I learn that Thierry Coulard's dog, a fine creature renowned for its sobriety, forgot itself one day and began to lap up a small puddle beneath the barrel, and either it had a seizure or was poisoned, because it fell down stiff as a board only escaping the claws of death thanks to an exceptionally sturdy constitution. They are holding their sides with mirth, I have trouble catching my breath.

An apple tart, with thin, crisp flaky pastry, and wedges of golden fruit insolently veiled beneath the discreet caramel sugar crystals. I finish the bottle. At five in the afternoon she serves me a coffee with calvados. The men get to their feet, slap me on the back and say they're going back to work, and that if I'm still there in the evening they'll be glad to see me. I hug them like brothers and promise to come back some day, with a good bottle.

It was there, beneath the centuries-old tree at the farm in Colleville, to the tune of pigs making a confounded racket (to the utmost delight of those who will tell the story one day), that I enjoyed one of my finest meals. The food was simple and delicious, but what I really devoured – to the point of relegating oysters, ham, asparagus and chicken to the rank of secondary accompaniments – was the truculence of my hosts' language; the syntax may have been brutally sloppy, but it was oh so warm in its juvenile authenticity. I feasted on their words, yes, the words flowing at that get-together of country brothers, the sort of words that, at times, delight one much more than the pleasures of the flesh. Words: repositories for singular realities which they then transform into moments in an anthology, magicians that change the face of reality by adorning it with the right to become memorable, to be placed in a library of memories. Life exists only by virtue of the osmosis of words and facts, where the former encase the latter in ceremonial dress. Thus, the words of my chance acquaintances, crowning the meal with an unprecedented grace, had almost formed the substance of my feast in spite of myself, and what I had enjoyed so merrily was the verb, not the flesh.

I am roused from my reverie by a dull sound, one that cannot fool my ears. Through my half-closed lids I can see Anna slipping furtively by in the corridor. This ability my wife has to move forward without walking, without altering her progress with the usual interruption of steps, has always made me suspect that such aristocratic fluidity was created for my sake alone. Anna . . . If you knew how happy I have been to redis-cover that labile afternoon, between eau-de-vie and forest, tossing my head back to gulp down the eternity of words! Perhaps those are the inner workings of my vocation, between what is said, and what is eaten . . . and the flavour, still, escapes me, dizzyingly . . . I am drawn by my thoughts towards my life in the provinces . . . a large house . . . long walks through the fields . . . the dog at my feet, joyful and innocent . . .

(Venus)

Rue de Grenelle, the Study

I am a primitive Venus, a small fertility goddess with a naked alabaster body: large, generous hips, a prominent belly and breasts falling to my rounded thighs, which lie one against the other in a somewhat comically shy attitude. A woman rather than a gazelle: everything in me invokes flesh, not contemplation. And yet, he looks at me, he never stops looking at me, the instant he lifts his eyes from his page, the instant he begins to meditate and sets his long dark gaze upon me without seeing me. Other times, however, he scrutinises me thoughtfully, trying to penetrate my immobile sculpture's soul, I can tell he is a whisker away from establishing contact, from guessing, conversing, and then suddenly he gives up and I have the exasperating feeling that I have just attended the performance of a man who is looking at himself in a two-way mirror, never suspecting for a moment that from behind the mirror, someone is observing him. And sometimes his fingertips graze over me, he rubs the folds of my splendid womanhood, wanders with his palms over my featureless face, and upon my ivory surface I can feel his power, all untamed emotional maladjustment. When he sits down at his desk and pulls the cord of the big copper lamp, and a ray of warm light flows onto my shoulders, I am reborn each time from this demiurgical light, I re-emerge from nowhere, and this is the way it is for him with the flesh-and-blood creatures who cross his path in life, they are absent from memory when he turns his back upon them and, when once again they enter the field of his perception, they offer him a presence he cannot grasp. He looks at them, too, without seeing them, apprehends them in a void, the way a blind man gropes before him, because he thinks he is grasping hold of something, when in fact he is merely stirring up evanescence, embracing the void. His watchful, intelligent eyes are separated from what they see by an invisible veil that hinders his judgement, renders opaque that which could, however, be so easily illuminated by his wit. And the veil is that of his rigidity, of the distraught autocrat, with his perpetual anxiety that the person opposite him might turn out to be something other than an object he can dismiss from his vision at leisure, and at the same time that this person might not be a freedom that could recognise his own . . .

When he looks for me, without ever finding me, when at last he resigns himself to lowering his eyes or to grabbing hold of the cord in order to annihilate my existence, he is fleeing, fleeing, fleeing the unbearable. How he desires other people; how he fears them.

Die, old man. There is no peace and there is no place for you in this life.

The Dog

Rue de Grenelle, the Bedroom

In the early hours of our companionship, I was relentlessly fascinated by the indisputable elegance with which he would lower his hindquarters; settled nicely between his rear paws, his tail sweeping the ground with the regularity of a metronome, his little hairless pink tummy folding softly beneath his downy chest, he would sit down vigorously and raise his moist hazelnut eyes to me, and often I thought I could see something else there besides mere appetite.

I had a dog. Or rather, a snout on paws. A little receptacle of anthropomorphic projections. A loyal companion. A tail that kept time with his emotions. An overexcited kangaroo at certain times of the day. A dog, as I said. When he first came to the house, his plump little folds of flesh could easily have inspired in me a sort of silly-making tenderness; but in the space of a few weeks the little round ball had become a slender little dog with a well-defined muzzle, clear, luminous eyes, an inquisitive nose, a powerful chest and well-muscled paws. He was a Dalmatian, and I'd baptised him Rhett, in honour of *Gone with the Wind*, my favourite film, because if I had been a woman, I would have been Scarlett – the one who survives in a world that is dying. His immaculate fur, with its meticulous sprinkling of black, was incredibly silky; as it happens, the Dalmatian is a very silky dog, both to look at and to touch. Not in an unctuous way, however: there was nothing complacent or sappy about the immediate sympathy that his physiognomy aroused, only a great propensity towards loving sincerity.

Moreover, when he tilted his muzzle to one side, his ears perked forward, falling in fluid flaps along his drooping chops, I understood how much the love one has for an animal is part of one's self-image; and I did not regret this, for in such moments he was utterly irresistible. And besides, there is no doubt that after a certain amount of cohabitation, man and beast borrow each other's failings. Rhett – who was, incidentally, rather poorly trained, that is to say not trained at all – was in fact afflicted with a pathology that hardly came as a surprise. If I qualified as gluttony the trait which ended up, in his case, more like obsessive bulimia, I would be falling far short of the truth. If a simple lettuce leaf fell to the floor, he would pounce upon it with an impressive nose dive that ended in a compact slide of his hindquarters, and then he would devour the leaf without even chewing it, in his fear of being tricked; I am convinced that it was only after the fact that he would identify what it was that he had caught. No doubt his motto was, Eat first, look later, and I often told myself that I was the owner of the only dog in the world who placed a higher price on his desire to eat than on the act of eating, for the greater part of his daily activity was spent in being where he might *hope* to happen upon some revolting crumb. Nevertheless, his ingeniousness did not extend to inventing subterfuges in order to procure some victuals; but he was master of the art of placing himself strategically in the exact spot where a forgotten sausage might be lured away from the grill, or a crushed potato crisp, vestige of a hasty pre-dinner drink, might escape the attention of the masters of the house. More seriously, his irrepressible passion for eating was eloquently (and somewhat dramatically) illustrated one Christmas in Paris, at my grandparents', where the meal, according to some antediluvian custom, would always finish with a Yule log lovingly prepared by my grandmother, a simple Swiss roll stuffed with a butter, coffee or chocolate cream – it may have been a simple Swiss roll but it was laden with the magnificence of successful endeavours. Rhett was in fine fettle and frolicked his way around the apartment, gathering caresses here, being surreptitiously fed there with some treat carelessly dropped onto the carpet behind my father's back, and so, from the beginning of the meal, he had been doing the rounds on a regular basis (corridor, living room, dining room, kitchen, corridor and so on) where he engaged in not a few generous licking sessions. It was my father's sister Marie who first noticed his absence. I realised at the same time as the others that indeed for quite a while we had not noticed the recurring wag of the white, quivering plume above the armchairs, which was the sign that the dog was going by. After a short lapse of time during which we became brutally aware, my father, mother and I, of the probable turn of events, we leapt to our feet as if propelled by a single spring, and rushed to the bedroom where, as a precaution, because she knew the little rascal and his love of anything remotely culinary, my grandmother had stored the very precious dessert.

The bedroom door was open. Someone (the guilty party was never identified), despite all the admonishments in the matter, had forgotten to close the door, and the dog, whom one could hardly expect to single-handedly resist his own nature, had quite naturally concluded that the Yule log belonged to him. My mother let out a cry of despair: a white-tailed eagle in distress surely does not produce such wrenching cries. Rhett, in all probability too heavy from his spoils to react in his usual fashion, that is, by rushing through people's legs in order to reach a more benign refuge, stood there next to the empty plate watching us with a gaze devoid of all expression, all expectation fulfilled. Empty, in fact, is not exactly the right word. With methodical application, certain he would not be interrupted too soon, he had attacked the Yule log from right to left, then from left to right, and so on across its entire length, until we finally got there and all that was left of the sweet butter triumph was a thin, elongated filament, and it would have been futile indeed to hope that something might be recovered, to find its way onto our plates. Like Penelope unravelling the yarn on her loom, row upon row along its length, from a cloth that was meant to be a tapestry, Rhett had put his industrious fangs to good use in order to fashion a busy little shuttle, weaving the pleasure of his connoisseur's stomach.

My grandmother had such a good laugh that the incident was transformed from galactic catastrophe to delicious anec- dote. This was another aspect of the woman's talent, the way she could see the salt of life in situations where others might see nothing but inconvenience. She wagered that the dog would be the instrument of his own punishment by virtue of the monumental indigestion which the ingurgitation of a pastry intended for fifteen people could not fail to provoke without delay. She was proven wrong. Despite the suspicious protuberance which could be observed for several hours in the region of his belly, Rhett digested his Christmas meal very well, aided by a deep siesta during which he could be heard cooing with pleasure from time to time, and he was not even terribly indignant when the next morning he came upon his empty bowl, a paltry retaliatory measure implemented by my father who, to say the least, had not appreciated the display of mischief.

Is there a moral to the story? I briefly begrudged Rhett for having deprived me of a pleasure foretold. But I had also laughed wholeheartedly at the sight of the serene disrespect the dog had manifested towards the relentless labours of my dragon of a grandmother. And above all, there was one thought that had crossed my mind and which I had found very heartening. Seated around the table for the occasion were so many of my relatives for whom I felt at best scorn, at worst animosity, that in the end it seemed to me a delightful conclusion that the cake which had been destined for their dreary taste buds had delighted my dog's instead, for I am sure he had all the talents of a true gourmet. I am not, however, one of those people who prefer their dog to a stranger; a dog is nothing more than a thing that moves, barks and wiggles, while wandering through the province of our daily life. But if one must display one's disgust for those who deserve it, it may as well be done via these amusing furry beasts: they may be insignificant, but they are also marvellously adept at innocently conveying mockery, in spite of themselves.

A gift, a clown, a clone: he was all those things at once. He was funny, with his merry figure of soft refinement; he offered himself by radiating the unaffected kindness of his puppy soul; he was a clone of my own self, but then not altogether: I no longer saw the dog in him, any more than I made him into a man. He was Rhett, Rhett above all, before being a dog, or an angel, or a beast, or a demon. But if I am speaking of him a few hours before my demise, it is because I have offended him by omitting him in my earlier evocation of natural fragrances. Indeed, Rhett was a source of olfactory delight all to himself. Yes, my dog, my Dalmatian, was a past master at sniffing out a scent; and believe it or not, on his neck and on the top of his well-shaped crown he smelled like the toasty aroma of brioche bread with butter and cherry-plum jam that would fill the kitchen in the morning. Thus, Rhett gave off the lovely smell of warm brioche, a yeasty scent, which immediately made you want to sink your teeth in, and just picture this: all day long, the dog would frolic everywhere around the house and in the garden; whether he was trotting, supremely busy, from the living room to the study, or galloping to the far end of the field in a crusade against three presumptuous crows, or fidgeting in the kitchen in hope of a tasty morsel, he always gave off the evocative aroma, and was thus a permanent living ode to the Sunday morning brioche: numb but content at the start of our day of rest, we would slip on a comfortable old cardigan and go down to make the coffee, one eye on the brown loaf sitting on the table. It's a delightful feeling to be not yet quite awake, taking a few silent moments to enjoy the fact of not being subject to the laws of work, rubbing your eyes in a display of sympathy for yourself and, when the palpable aroma of hot coffee rises, you finally sit down before your steaming bowl and give a friendly squeeze to the brioche as you tear it apart; then you slowly dip a piece in the bowl of caster sugar in the middle of the table and with your eyes half closed you acknowledge – and no need to tell yourself as much – the bittersweet quality of happiness. It is all of this that Rhett could evoke with his fragrant presence, and if I loved him as I did it was also surely for the way he came and went like some itinerant *boulangerie*.

As I reminisce about Rhett, reliving these adventures I haven't thought about in so long, there is one abandoned aroma I have been able to recapture: that of warm and fragrant pastry, nestled in my dog's head. An aroma and therefore other similar memories – mornings in America, and the buttered toast that I used to gobble down, astounded by the symbiosis between bread and butter when they have been toasted *together.*

(Anna)

Rue de Grenelle, the Corridor

What is to become of me, my God, what is to become of me? I have no more strength, I cannot breathe, I have been emptied out, bled dry . . . I know that they don't understand, except Paul perhaps, I know what they are thinking . . . Jean, Laura, Clémence, where are you? Why this silence, why this distance, why all these misunderstandings, when we could have been so happy, the five of us? All you see is a cantankerous, authoritarian old man, you've never seen anyone but a tyrant, an oppressor, a despot who made life impossible for you, and for me – you set yourself up as knights in attendance who would console me in my distress as an abandoned wife and, in the end, I have not disabused you, I let you embellish my daily life with your laughter, as loving, comforting children, I have silenced my passion, silenced my reasons. I have silenced my own self.

I have always known what sort of life we would lead together. From the very first day, I could see that for him, far away from me, there would be banquets, and other women, and the career of a charmer with insane, miraculous talent; a prince, a lord constantly hunting outside his own walls, a man who, from one year to the next, would become ever more distant, would no longer even see me, would pierce my haunted soul with his falcon's eyes in order to embrace a view that was beyond my sight. I always knew this, and it didn't matter. The only thing that mattered were the times when he came back, and he always came back, and that was enough for me, I would be the woman to whom one returns, unfailingly, however absent-mindedly and vaguely. If you knew him, you would understand . . . If you knew the nights I have spent in his arms, trembling with excitement, transfixed with desire, crushed by his royal weight, his divine strength, I was happy, so happy, like the woman in love in her harem on the evenings when it is her turn, when she receives, reverently, the pearls of his gaze – because she lives for him alone, for his embrace, for his light. Perhaps he finds her tame, coy, childish; elsewhere, he has other lovers, tigresses, sensual felines, lustful panthers, with whom he roars with pleasure, in a debauchery of moans, of erotic gymnastics, and when it's all over, he feels as if he has reinvented the world, he is inflated with pride, inflated with faith in his own virility – but, in fact, she takes her sensual pleasure on a deeper level, a mute pleasure, she gives herself, gives herself entirely, receives religiously and it is in a church-like silence that she attains the pinnacle, almost without anyone noticing, because she has no need of anything else: his presence, his kisses. She is happy.

And so her children . . . she loves them, obviously. The joys of motherhood, of bringing them up, are things she has known; as well as the horror of having to raise children who are unloved by their father, the torture of watching them gradually learn to hate him, because he looks down on them, because he has abandoned her . . . But above all, she feels guilty because she loves them less than she loves him, because she was not able, was not willing to protect them from the man she was waiting for with all her waking energy, and there was no room left for anything else, no room left for them . . . If I had left, if I had been able to hate him too, then I might have saved them, they would have been released from the prison into which I cast them, the prison of my resignation, of my mad desire for my own torturer . . . I raised my children to love their tormenter . . . And today I am weeping tears of blood, because he is dying, he is leaving . . .

I remember how splendid we were, I held your arm, I smiled in the gentle evening air, in my black silk gown, I was your wife and everyone turned to look at us, murmuring, an appreciative whispering following in our footsteps, it followed us everywhere, like a light breeze, eternal . . . Don't die, please don't die . . . I love you . . .

Toast

Rue de Grenelle, the Bedroom

It was during a sojourn abroad occasioned by a seminar. I was already well known at the time, and I had been invited by the French community in San Francisco, where I chose to stay with a French journalist who lived near the Pacific Ocean, in a neighbourhood to the southwest of the city. On the very first morning I was ravenous and my hosts were taking too long, for my liking, over their discussion of where to take me for 'the breakfast of a lifetime'. Through the open window, on a little prefab building, I could see a sign that said 'John's Ocean Beach Cafe', and I decided it would be good enough for me.

From the start, I was beguiled by the door. The 'open' sign, hanging on the frame from a little golden chain, went very well with the gleaming copper knob and made arrival at the café particularly welcoming, in an inexplicable way – it all made such an agreeable impression on me. But when I went into the main room, I was carried away. This was just as I had dreamt America would be, and despite all my expectations, flouting my certainty that once I was there I would revise all my clichés, it was exactly as I had imagined: a large rectangular room with wooden tables and booths covered in red leatherette; on the walls were photos of actors, a poster from *Gone with the Wind* with Scarlett and Rhett on the boat taking them to New Orleans; a vast, well-polished wooden counter cluttered with butter, maple-syrup dispensers and ketchup bottles. A blonde waitress with a strong Slavic accent came over to us with coffee pot in hand; behind the bar, John, the chef, looking like an

Italian Mafioso, was busy grilling hamburgers with a disdainful sneer and a cynical expression. The interior of the café belied the exterior: everything bore a patina of age, worn furniture and a divine aroma of food frying. Oh, John! I had a look at the menu, chose the Scrambled Eggs with Sausage and John's Special Potatoes, and before long there arrived, in addition to a steaming cup of undrinkable coffee, a plate or rather a platter overflowing with scrambled eggs and potatoes sautéed in garlic, topped with three greasy little aromatic sausages, while the pretty Russian waitress set down next to all this a smaller plate piled high with buttered toast, accompanied by a pot of blueberry jam. People say Americans are fat because they eat too much and badly. This is true, but one should not include their gargantuan breakfasts in this incrimination. I am inclined to think that, on the contrary, they are exactly what a man needs to face the day, and our stingy little French breakfasts – given the spinelessness clearly imbued with snobbery with which anything salty or porky is shunned – constitute an insult to the requisites of the body.

The moment I bit into the slice of toast, utterly sated after doing justice to my bountiful plate down to the very last morsel, I was overcome with an inexpressible sense of well-being. Why is it that in France we obstinately refrain from buttering our bread until after it has been toasted? The reason the two entities should be subjected together to the flickering flame is that in this intimate moment of burning they attain an unequalled complicity. The butter loses some of its creamy consistency, but nevertheless is not as liquid as when it is melted on its own, in a bain-marie or a saucepan. Likewise, the toast is spared a somewhat dreary dryness, and becomes a moist, warm substance, neither sponge nor bread but something in between, ready to tantalise one's taste buds with its contemplative delicacy.

*

It is terrible how close I feel. Bread, brioche . . . it seems that at last I am heading down the right path, the one which will lead to my truth. Or have I been induced in error yet again – the wrong track leading me astray, convincing me all the better to disappoint me, to laugh sarcastically at my undoing? I shall try other alternatives. Time to take a gamble.

(Rick)

Rue de Grenelle, the Bedroom

S o here I am, lounging in my basket, or sprawled on the
sofa feeling feline – have you ever seen such purrfect
style?!

My name is Rick. My master is generally inclined to give his
pets names from films, but I must hasten to point out that I am
his favourite. Indeed I am. Many cats have passed through here
over the years: a few of them unfortunately were not robust
enough and they quickly disappeared, others were victims of
tragic accidents (like the year they had to replace the drainpipe
that had given way under the weight of a very sweet little
white cat called Scarlett), and there were others with greater
longevity, but now I am the only one left, and here I am,
nineteen years I've been knocking about as head tomcat on the
Persian rugs of my abode; just me, the favourite, the master's
alter ego, the one and only, to whom he declared his thoughtful, undying love one day when I was stretched out on the desk
across his latest restaurant review, beneath the big warm lamp.
'Rick,' he said, ruffling the fur at the base of my spine, 'Rick,
you're my favourite, oh yes, what a fine cat you are, aren't you,
now . . . I'm not angry with you, you can even tear up this
paper, I'll never get angry with you . . . who's a fine tom with
his buccaneer's whiskers . . . his silky fur . . . look at those
Olympian muscles . . . that Herculean back . . . those iridescent
opal eyes . . . yes, my fine kitty . . . my one and only . . .'

Why Rick? you may ask. I myself often wondered, but as I
have no words with which to formulate the question, it went

unheeded until one December evening about ten years ago, when that little red-headed woman who used to come to the house to have tea with the Maître asked, as she gently stroked my neck, where my name had come from. (I liked her, that lady, she always had a slightly musky aroma about her, very unusual for a woman, as most of her sex are inevitably smeared with heavy, heady perfumes, lacking that little scent of venison in which a cat – a real cat – can find just what he's looking for.) He replied, 'It's after the character Rick in *Casablanca*, he's a man who knows how to give up a woman because he would rather have his freedom.' I could sense that she stiffened a little. But I could also appreciate that aura of manly seduction with which the Maître gratified me through his offhand reply.

Of course today none of that matters any more. Today the Maître is going to die. I know he is, I heard Chabrot tell him so, and when he had left, the Maître took me on his lap, looked me in the eyes (they must really have been pitiful, my poor tired eyes, and it's not because cats don't cry that they don't know how to show they are sad and he said, sorrowfully, 'Never listen to doctors, sweetheart.' But I can see that it's the end. His, and mine, because I've always known we would have to die together. And so while his right hand is on my docile tail and I've got my pads planted on the plumped-up eiderdown, I can reminisce.

It was always like this. I would hear his quick steps on the tiles in the entrance, and very soon he'd be coming up the steps two by two. I would instantly jump up onto my velvet paws and make a beeline for the hall and there, on the somewhat ochre kilim, between the coat rack and the marble console table, I would wait obediently.

He would open the door, remove his overcoat, hang it up with an abrupt gesture, see me at last and then lean over to caress me with a smile. Anna would arrive soon after, but he didn't look at her, and went on stroking me, gently petting me.

'Has he lost weight, the cat, do you think, Anna?' he would ask, a touch of concern in his voice. 'Of course not, dearest, of course not.' I would follow him into his study, then perform his favourite number (crouch down, leap and land noiselessly, as soft as leather, on the morocco-bound blotter). 'Good boy, come over here, come and tell me everything that's been happening all this time . . . Yes . . . I've got the devil's own amount of work here . . . but you don't care and you're absolutely right . . . mmm, feel that silky little belly . . . there, stretch out over there so I can get some work done . . .'

Never again will there be the scratching of his pen on the white sheet, never again those afternoons with the rain pounding on the windowpane, while next to him in the muffled comfort of his impenetrable study I would grow languid, faithfully accompanying the gestation of his grandiose *oeuvre*. Never again.

Whisky

Rue de Grenelle, the Bedroom

My grandpa had been in the war with him. They hadn't had much to say to each other since that memorable time, but it had sealed between them an indestructible friendship which would not cease even upon my grandfather's death. Gaston Bienheureux – that was his name – would continue to visit his friend's widow for as long as she was still alive, and went so far as to display the silent tact of dying a few weeks after she did, his task accomplished.

Sometimes he came to Paris on business and he never failed to stop off at his friend's with a little crate of the latest vintage. But twice a year, at Easter and All Saints' Day, it was Grandpa who 'went down' to Burgundy, alone, without his wife, for three days which we assumed were well watered, and he was always taciturn upon his return, deigning only to articulate that they had 'had a good talk'.

When I was fifteen he took me with him. Burgundy is reputed above all for its wines from the Côte, the narrow verdant strip of land which stretches from Dijon to Beaune through an impressive palette of prestigious names: Gevrey- Chambertin, Nuits-Saint-Georges, Aloxe-Corton, and, further south, Pommard, Monthélie and Meursault, almost exiled to the border of the county. Gaston Bienheureux was not one to envy those well-off sorts. In Irancy he was born, in Irancy he lived, in Irancy he would die. In this little village in the Yonne region, nestled in a farandole of hills and entirely devoted to the grape which prospers in its generous soil, there is no envy of faraway neighbours, for the nectar lovingly produced there does not seek competition. It knows its strengths, it has its qualities: there is nothing more it needs in order to endure.

The French are often, when it comes to wine, so formal that they border on the ridiculous. My father had taken me, several months earlier, to visit the cellars of the Château de Meursault: so much splendour! The arches and vaulted ceilings, the pomp of the labels, the coppered gleam of the racks, and the crystal glasses all spoke of the quality of the wine, but were hindrances to my pleasure upon tasting it. All these luxurious intrusions of decor and decorum were interferences, and I could not determine whether it was the liquid or the surroundings that were teasing my tongue with an extravagant stimulus. To be honest, I was not yet terribly sensitive to the charms of wine, but I was only too aware that a man of quality is obliged to appreciate tasting it on a daily basis, and so, in the hope that things would eventually head down the right path, I confessed to no one that all I gleaned from the exercise was a very mediocre satisfaction. Since that time, naturally, I have been inducted into the brotherhood of wine, I have come to understand – and reveal to others – the power of a full-bodied vintage pulsating in one's mouth, flooding it with a bouquet of tannin where the flavour is increased tenfold. But at the time I was too immature to measure up to wine, and I drank it somewhat reticently, waiting impatiently for it to share with me the talents for which it is renowned. Therefore, what I looked forward to in my grandpa's treat was not so much the alcoholic promises it concealed as the pleasure of his company and the discovery of an unfamiliar countryside.

From the start I liked the landscape, but also Gaston's wine cellar, a place without frills, a simple large damp cellar with a beaten-earth floor and cob walls. Here there were neither vaults nor arches; nor was there a chateau to greet the customer, only a pretty Burgundian house blooming with courtesy and discreet by vocation; a few ordinary stem glasses placed on a barrel at the entrance to the cellar. That is where, no sooner had we stepped out of the car, we began our tasting.

How they talked, on and on. Glass after glass, as they went through the bottles the winemaker opened one after the other, with total disregard for the spittoons placed here and there in the room for those who wanted to taste without fear of getting drunk; they drank methodically, accompanying the purely phatic rehashing of clearly imaginary memories with impressive amounts of liquid. I was no longer feeling very robust myself when Gaston, who thus far had only acknowledged me somewhat absent-mindedly, looked me over more sharply and said to my grandfather, 'The lad doesn't care for wine much, now, does he?' I was too tipsy to protest my innocence. What's more, with his overalls, wide black braces, red plaid shirt as bright as his nose and cheeks, and his black beret, I really liked the man, and didn't want to lie to him. So I did not contradict him.

Every man, in his way, is master of his castle. The coarsest peasant, the most uncultured winemaker, the most miserable employee, the shabbiest shopkeeper, the greatest pariah among all those who have been excluded from the consideration of society, rejected lock stock and barrel; the simplest of men, therefore, always have in their possession their very own genius, the one that will ensure them of their hour of glory. All the more so someone like Gaston, who was not a pariah. This simple worker, who may have been a prosperous tradesman but remained a peasant at heart, isolated on his few acres of vineyard, suddenly became for me a prince among princes, because in any activity, whether noble or reviled, there is always room for an all-powerful flash of realisation.

'Shouldn't you teach him something about life, Albert?' he asked. 'Do you think the kid would be up for some DTH?' And my grandfather laughed quietly. 'You see, lad,' continued

Gaston, inspired by the imminent prospect of furthering my education, 'everything you've tasted here today is good stuff, the real thing. But a winemaker doesn't sell everything: as you might suspect, he keeps some stuff for himself, for his thirst, not for trade' – his good-natured mug was split ear to ear by a smile worthy of a crafty fox – 'so he always keeps some DTH on hand, some "down the hatch". And when he has people round, friends, I should say, well, he dips into his DTH.' He suddenly interrupted the tippling that was already well under way. 'Come with me, come on then,' he said impatiently, as I rose unsteadily to my feet. Giving him a grim look, my tongue coated with the devious ways of drink, I followed him to the back of the cellar and, although I was greatly intrigued by this new concept, the DTH, which was bound to offer undreamt-of glimpses into the lifestyle of gentlemen of taste, I expected it to lead to still more glug-glugging of wine, a prospect that filled me with a certain amount of apprehension. 'Since you're still a bit on the young side for the serious things of life,' he continued, stopping in front of a massive cupboard armed with an enormous padlock, 'and with the parents you have, you can't expect too much either' – he slipped my grandfather a gaze that left no doubt about what he was implying, and Albert said not a word – 'to my way of thinking it's time to blow out your cobwebs with something a bit more astringent. What I'm going to dig out here for you from behind the firewood is something I'm sure you've never drunk. It's good stuff. This will be your baptism. I'll say it again: you're in for a true education.'

Out of an unfathomably deep pocket he pulled a very heavy set of keys, put one of them into the enormous lock, and turned. My grandpa's expression instantly became more serious. Warned by this sudden solemnity, I sniffed nervously, straightened my spine, which had become seriously impaired by our tippling, and waited with considerable apprehension

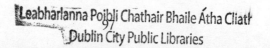

while Gaston, with a meaningful gesture, took from the safe a bottle wrapped in black that most definitely was not wine, and a large, squat, unadorned glass.

This was the DTH. He ordered his whisky from Scotland, from one of the best distilleries in the country. The owner was a chap he'd known in Normandy, just after the war, with whom he'd quickly discovered a shared affinity for liquids rated by degrees. Every year a crate of the precious whisky came to join the handful of bottles of wine he put aside for personal use. And from varietals to peat, from ruby to amber, and from alcohol to alcohol, he reconciled the two before and during meals that he himself qualified as profoundly European.

'I sell some good things, but the best go down my hatch.' The way he treated the few bottles set aside from the grape harvest, and his friend Mark's whisky (to his regular guests he only served a very good whisky bought locally, which was to the Scotsman's whisky what a tomato in a can is to its rival in the vegetable garden), caused him to rise all at once in my adolescent's esteem, which already assumed that greatness and expertise are to be measured by exceptions and not by rules, even if they were rules made by kings. With his private little cellar Gaston Bienheureux had just become, in my eyes, a potential artist. Subsequently I never failed to suspect all the restaurateurs in whose establishments I dined of displaying on their tables no more than the minor works of their industry, and of keeping for themselves, in the intimacy of their culinary alcoves, victuals that were worthy of a pantheon and inaccessible to ordinary mortals. But for the moment I was hardly preoccupied by such philosophical consideration. I stared dumbly at the bronze liquid as he poured out a meagre portion and, filled with misgivings, I sought in my deepest soul the courage to confront it.

To start with, the unfamiliar aroma unsettled me beyond anything I thought possible. Such formidable aggressiveness, such a muscular, abrupt explosion, dry and fruity at the same time, like a charge of adrenalin that has deserted the tissues where it ordinarily resides in order to evaporate upon the surface of the nose, a gaseous concentration of sensorial precipices . . . Stunned, I discovered that I liked this blunt whiff of incisive fermentation.

Like some ethereal marchioness, I cautiously ventured my lips into the peaty magma and . . . what a violent effect! An explosion of piquancy and seething elements suddenly detonates in my mouth; my organs no longer exist, no more palate or cheeks or saliva, only the ravaging sensation of some telluric warfare raging inside me. In raptures, I allowed the first mouthful to linger for a moment on my tongue, while concentric undulations continued to engage it for a long while. That is the first way to drink whisky: absorb it ferociously, inhaling its pungent, unforgiving taste. The second mouthful, on the other hand, was undertaken precipitously; as soon as it had gone down, it took a moment to warm my solar plexus – but what warmth it was! The stereotypical gesture of the man who drinks strong spirits – swallowing down the object of his desire in one gulp, then waiting, then closing his eyes from the shock and exhaling a sigh of mingled ease and commotion – offers a second manner of drinking whisky, where the taste buds are almost insensitive because the alcohol is merely passing through one's throat, and the plexus, perfectly sensitive, is suddenly overwhelmed by heat as if a bomb of ethylic plasma had landed there. It heats, and heats again, it disconcerts and rouses. It feels good. It is a sun whose blessed rays assure the body of its beaming presence.

Thus it was in the heart of wine-growing Burgundy that I drank my first whisky and experienced for the first time the power it has to wake the dead. With this added irony: the fact that Gaston himself led me to this discovery should have put me on the path of my true passion. Yet throughout my career

I have never considered whisky to be anything more than a drink which, however delightful, is nevertheless of secondary importance: only the gold of wine could deserve my praise and the most significant prophecies of my *oeuvre*. Alas . . . it is only now that I understand: wine is the refined jewel that only a grown woman will prefer to the sparkling glossy trinkets adored by little girls. I learned to love what was worthy but in doing so I neglected to entertain the sudden passion that had no need of education. I truly love only beer and whisky – even though I do acknowledge that wine is divine. And as it has been decreed that today will be little more than a long series of acts of contrition, here is yet another: oh, Mephistophelean whisky, I loved you from the first swig, and betrayed you from the second – but nowhere else did I ever find, amidst the tyranny of flavours imposed upon me by my position, such a nuclear expansion capable of blasting my jaw away with delight . . .

Desolation: I have been laying siege to my lost flavour in the wrong citadel . . . It is not to be found in the wind or heather of a desolate moor, nor in a deep loch or a dark stone wall. All of that is lacking in indulgence, in affability, in moderation. Ice, not fire: I find myself trapped down the wrong impasse.

(Laure)

Nice

On est bien peu de chose, et mon amie la rose me l'a dit ce matin . . . My God, what a sad song . . . I am sad myself . . . and weary, so weary . . .

I was born into an old French family where values still remain what they have always been. A family of granite rigidity. It would never have crossed my mind that these values might be questioned: an idiotic and old-fashioned youth – somewhat romantic, somewhat diaphanous – spent waiting for Prince Charming and exhibiting my cameo profile whenever a worldly occasion arose. And then I got married, and quite naturally it meant the passage from the protection of my parents to that of my husband, and the dashing of my hopes, and the insignificance of life as a woman who is kept back for ever in childhood, a life devoted to bridge parties and receptions, utterly unaware that there might actually be something better to do.

And then I met him. I was still young and beautiful, a slender doe, too easy a prey. The excitement of secrecy, the adrenalin of adultery, the fever of forbidden sex: I had found my prince, I had drugged my life, on the sofa I played my role, languishing and lovely; I let him admire my willowy, racy beauty, at last I was alive, I existed, and in his eyes I became a goddess, I became Venus.

Of course, he didn't really want anything to do with a sentimental little girl. What for me had been transgression was for him merely futile entertainment, a charming distraction. Indifference is far more cruel than hatred: from non-being I had come, to non-being I would return. To my sullen husband, to my bleary frivolousness, to the eroticism of an innocent young thing, to the empty thoughts of a graceful silly goose: my cross to bear, my Waterloo.

Let him die, then.

Ice Cream

Rue de Grenelle, the Bedroom

What I liked about Marquet was her generosity. She didn't seek to innovate at any cost – a tactic many great chefs resort to in order to ward off the criticism that they are afraid of change – and while she did not rest on her laurels with her existing accomplishments, she only worked relentlessly because, in the end, it was her nature, and she liked what she was doing. Thus, when dining in her restaurant, you could just as easily romp your way through a menu that was perpetually youthful as order a dish from an earlier era, which she would prepare with all the good grace of a prima donna cajoled through flattery to provide an encore of one of the arias that made her famous.

I had been feasting at her place for twenty years. Of all the great chefs I have had the honour of frequenting on intimate terms, she was the only one who truly embodied my ideal of creative perfection. She never disappointed me: her dishes always baffled me to the bone, to the point of inducing a fit, perhaps precisely because her even touch and the originality of her perpetually inventive provender came so naturally.

That July evening, I had sat down at *my* table outside, as over-excited as a mischievous child. The Marne was lapping gently at my feet. The white stone of the old restored mill, halfway between land and river, eaten away in places by a soft green moss that found its way into the slightest crack, was glowing gently in the early darkness. Before long, the terraces would be lit. I have always had a particular fondness for fertile countryside, where a river, a spring or a stream, flowing across the meadow, confers upon the surroundings the serenity of uliginous atmospheres. A house by the water: crystalline tranquillity, the lure of still water, the mineral indifference of waterfalls, no sooner here than gone again, serving forthwith to make all human concerns seem relative. But on that particular day, I felt incapable of savouring the charms of the place, almost reclusive, and I waited with relative patience for the mistress of the premises to arrive. Which she did almost at once.

'Well,' I said, 'this evening I would like a rather particular supper.' And I enumerated my requests.

Menu. 1982: *Sea urchin royale with Sansho, saddle of hare, rabbit kidneys and liver with winkles. Buckwheat pancake.* 1979: *Cod in an agria macaire; violet maco from the Midi; plump Gillardeau oysters and grilled foie gras. Mackerel bouillon laced with leeks.* 1989: *Thick chunks of turbot cooked in a casserole with aromatic herbs, deglazed with homemade cider. Quarters of Comice pears with verts de concombre.* 1996: *Pastis of Gauthier pigeon with mace, dried fruit and foie gras with radishes.* 1988: *Madeleines with tonka beans.*

It was an anthology. In one single clutch of eternity I had gathered together that which years of culinary spiritedness had created in the way of timeless blandishments: from the shapeless accumulation of dishes I was extracting a handful of veritable nuggets, the contiguous pearls of a goddess's necklace, in order to make them into a work of legend.

A moment of triumph. She looked at me for an instant, flabbergasted, the time it took to *understand*; lowered her gaze onto my empty, waiting plate; then, slowly, training an ever so appreciative gaze upon me – full of praise, admiring and respectful all at the same time – she nodded her head and puckered her lips in a pout of deferential homage. 'Well, yes, of course,' she said. 'Of course, it's proof that . . .'

Naturally, it was a feast worthy of an anthology, and it was perhaps the only time during our long cohabitation as food lovers that we were truly united in the fervour of the meal, neither critic nor cook, only high-flying connoisseurs sharing their allegiance to a same emotion. But while this memory of noble lineage may flatter above all my self-importance as a creator, that is not the reason I have caused it to re-emerge from the mists of my unconsciousness.

Madeleines of tonka beans, or the art of the offhand short cut! It would be an insult to assume that a dessert chez Marquet could consist of nothing more than a few skinny madeleines set on a plate and sprinkled with beans. The pastry was hardly more than a pretext, that of a psalm – sweet, honeyed, fondant and dripping – where, in the mad confusion of sponge, candied fruits, icings, crêpes, chocolate, sabayons, red berries, ice creams and sorbets, a progressive passage from hot to cold was being explored by my expert tongue; it clucked with compulsive satisfaction, it danced a devilish jig at the merriest of balls. I favoured ice cream and sorbet, in particular. I adore ice cream: frozen cream saturated with milk, fat, artificial flavours, bits of fruit, coffee beans, rum; Italian gelati solid as velvet spiralled with vanilla, strawberry or chocolate; ice cream sundaes crumbling under the weight of whipped cream, peaches, almonds and coulis of all sorts; simple ice lollies with a coating that is crunchy, fine and firm all at once, that you eat in the street, between meetings, or in the evening in summer in front of the television, when it has become clear that this is the only way to make yourself feel a little cooler, a little less thirsty; and finally the sorbets, the triumphant synthesis of ice and fruit, robust refreshment that evaporates in your mouth in a glacier's flow. The plate that had been set down in front of me contained examples of her industry: one was a tomato sorbet, another was classical, with wild berries and fruit, and a third one, finally, was orange.

In the simple word 'sorbet,' there is already an entire world. Try saying this out loud: 'Would you like an ice cream?' then immediately following with 'What about a sorbet?' and notice the difference. It's a bit like saying, as you open the door, in an offhand way, 'I'm going out to buy a cake,' whereas you could very well, without being so casual or banal, have ventured a little 'I'm going to get some patisseries' (and mind you detach each syllable: not 'patissries' but 'pa-tis-se-ries'), and, with the magic of a somewhat outdated, precious word you can create, at lesser cost, a world of old-style harmony. Thus, if you suggest 'sorbet' where others might merely be thinking 'ice cream' (which, very often, for the layman includes preparations made from milk or water), you have already opted for lightness, already chosen refinement, you are offering airy vistas while refusing a heavy land-bound trek with closed horizons. Airy, indeed: a sorbet is airy, almost immaterial, it froths ever so slightly as it makes contact with your warmth and then, vanquished, squeezed, liquefied, it evaporates down your throat and all it leaves on the tongue is the charming reminiscence of the fruit and water which once flowed there.

Thus I set upon the orange sorbet, tasted it as a man in the know, certain of what I was about to discover but attentive all the same to what were ever-changing sensations. And then something stopped me. I had tasted the other iced waters with the peace of mind of a connoisseur. But this sorbet, this orange one, was a cut above all the others, with its extravagant texture, its excessive aqueousness, as if someone had just filled a little bowl with a bit of water and a squeezed orange which had then been placed in the freezer for the regulation amount of time, producing these fragrant icy chunks, lumpy just as any impure liquid one tries to freeze can be, and which remind us strongly of the taste of the crumbly crushed snow we ate as children, with our hands, on days when the sky was a deep cold and we were playing outdoors. That was also my grandmother's opinion in the summer when at times it was so hot that I would tuck my head into the door of the freezer and, sweating and cursing, she would twist heavy dripping rags around her neck, which also served to slay a few lazy flies stuck together in places they shouldn't be. When the ice had set, she would turn the basin over, shake it vigorously above a bowl, crush the orangey mass and serve us a ladleful in a large goblet that we would seize as if it were a holy relic. And I realised that, in the end, all this banquet was for one thing alone: to reach the moment of the sorbet à l'orange, my childhood stalactites; to feel, tonight of all nights, the worth and truth of my gastronomic attachments.

Later, in the half darkness, I asked Marquet in a whisper, 'How do you do it, your sorbet, the sorbet à l'orange?'

She turned halfway on the pillow; light locks of hair curled around my shoulder.

'The way my grandmother does,' she answered, with a brilliant smile.

I'm nearly there. Fire . . . ice. Cream!

(Marquet)

Maison Marquet, near Meaux

No doubt about it, he was a regular bastard. He has consumed both my self and my cuisine with the presumptuousness of a common lout, as if it were only natural for Marquet to bow down before him, offering her dishes and her buttocks from the very first visit . . . A regular bastard, but we had some good times together, and that's something he can't take away from me, because what is mine, for good, is the thrill of conversing with a true genius of the food world, and of taking my pleasure with an exceptional lover; and still I remain a free woman, a proud woman . . .

Still, if he had been free, and if he had been the sort of man who might make of a woman something other than a tart available at all hours of the day – who knows . . . But then he wouldn't have been the same man, would he?

Mayonnaise

Rue de Grenelle, the Bedroom

There is nothing more delightful than to see the order of the world bend to one's desires. What unprecedented licence, to penetrate a temple of haute cuisine in the unbridled felicity of being able to taste each and every dish. The hidden frisson when the maître d' draws near with muffled footsteps; his impersonal gaze, a fragile yet successful compromise between respect and discretion, is a tribute to one's social capital. You are nobody because you are somebody; here, no one will spy on you, no one will try to pigeonhole you. The fact that you have been allowed to enter the premises is proof enough of who you are. A modest little tug at the heart as you open the menu, printed on a grainy vellum like a damask napkin of yore. Your astonishment expertly tempered as you feel your way for the first time through the whispered offer of dishes. Your gaze slips, refuses for a while to be caught by any particular ode, merely catches a few voluptuous fragments on the wing, frolics about in the luxurious profusion of terms you seize upon at random. Culotte of baby veal . . . pistachio cassata . . . wedge of angler fish on a bed of scampi . . . *galinette de palangre* . . . au naturel . . . amber gelée with aubergine. . . seasoned with Cremona mustard . . . a shallot confit . . . poached bass marinière . . . iced sabayon . . . in a grape must . . . blue lobster . . . breast of Peking duck . . . A first nibble of ecstasy at last when the magic takes over and devours your attention with a single line:

109

Pan-roasted breast of Peking duck rubbed with berbère; grapefruit crumble à la Jamaïque with shallot confit.

You repress any untimely salivation, your ability to concentrate has reached its summit. You are in possession of the symphony's dominant note.

It is not so much the duck or its berbère and grapefruit which have electrified you in this way, even if they are glazed with the promise of a dish whose key is sunny, spicy, and sweet, and whose hues range from almond to bronze to gold. But the shallot confit, instantly aromatic and fondant, pricking your still-virgin tongue with the anticipated savour of a melange of fresh ginger, marinated onion and musk, is titillating your appetite – and this is all it wants, after all – with its refinement and extravagance. On its own, however, this dish would not have been decisive; it required the incomparable poetry of 'pan-roasted', evoking in an olfactory cascade the aroma of fowl grilled in the open air at a cattle market, the sensorial pandemonium of Chinese bazaars, the irresistible conjunction of crispness and succulence when the meat is firm and juicy inside its crusty skin, the familiar mystery of the pan itself, neither a spit nor a grill, lulling the duck as it cooks; all of this is required, and the combination of odour and taste, to determine your choice on this particular day. All that remains is to embroider upon the theme.

How many times have I immersed myself in a menu the way one immerses oneself in the unknown? It would be pointless to try to work out such a figure. Every time, I have found my pleasure intact. But never has it been as acute as on that day when, by the stoves of the chef Lessière, in the holy of holies of gastronomic exploration, I turned away from a menu whose delights were deafening to wallow in the debauchery of simple mayonnaise.

*

I had dipped my finger into it, casually, in passing, the way you let your hand trail in fresh water from a drifting boat. We were talking together about his new menu, it was afternoon, between two waves of fellow diners, and in his kitchen I felt just as I used to in my grandmother's: I was a familiar stranger, allowed into the harem. What I tasted surprised me. This was indeed mayonnaise, and that was precisely what troubled me; a sheep that had lost its way amidst a pride of lions, this traditional condiment looked utterly and ridiculously archaic. 'What is this?' I asked, implying, how did a simple housewife's mayonnaise end up here? 'Well, it's mayonnaise,' he replied with a laugh. 'Don't tell me you don't know what mayonnaise is.' 'Mayonnaise just like that, the basic recipe?' I was quite unnerved.'Yes, the basic one. I don't know of any better way to make it. An egg, some oil, salt and pepper.' I insisted. 'And what is it meant to go with?' He looked at me carefully. 'I'll tell you,' he replied slowly, 'I'll tell you what it is meant to go with.' He ordered a kitchen boy to bring him some vegetables and some cold roast pork , and set about his task at once, peeling the vegetables.

I had forgotten, I had forgotten that in his position as *maître d'œuvre* and not critic he was obliged never to forget what we wrongly refer to as 'the basics' of cooking, and which comprise, if anything, the essential framework, and he had taken it upon himself to remind me, through a somewhat scornful lesson that he was giving me as a favour – for critics and chefs are like dishcloths and napkins: they complement each other, spend time together, work together, but in their heart of hearts, they do not like one another.

Carrots, celery, cucumbers, tomatoes, peppers, radishes, cauliflower and broccoli: he had cut them all lengthwise, or at any rate those that he could cut lengthwise, in other words all but the last two which, although flowery, could be taken by the stem, somewhat in the manner in which one grabs hold of the

111

hilt of a sword. To all this he added a few thin slices of roast pork, cold and succulent. We began to dip.

No one will ever manage to banish from my thoughts the notion that raw food with mayonnaise is somehow deeply sexual. The hard vegetable insinuating its way into the unctuousness of the cream; unlike many other preparations, here there is no chemistry causing each of the two foodstuffs to sacrifice a part of its nature and espouse that of the other, thus becoming through osmosis, like bread and butter, a new and wonderful substance. In this case, mayonnaise and vegetables remain perennial, each identical to its own self but, as in the carnal act, hopelessly ecstatic at being together. As for the meat, it nevertheless does obtain something more: its texture is elastic and porous, it yields to the bite and fills with mayonnaise in such a way that what one is chewing on, without false modesty, is something firm at heart that has been drizzled with a velvety moisture. Add to this the delicacy of a smooth flavour, for there is nothing biting about mayonnaise, no hot spiciness – like water, it surprises one's mouth with its affable neutrality; then come the exquisite nuances of the spread of vegetables: insolent tang of radishes and cauliflower, watery sweetness of the tomato, discreet acidity of broccoli, generosity of the carrot upon the tongue, the crunchy liquorice hints of celery . . . a treat fit for a king.

But just as I am recalling this incongruous meal – it was like a summer picnic by the woods, one of those perfect days when the sun is shining, there is a gentle breeze, and life seems to be decked out in clichés – a new memory has come to supersede it, and my reminiscences are suddenly illuminated with a deep authenticity, causing a turbulence of emotions to rise in my heart like bubbles of air forcing their way to the surface of the water which, when they break free, will explode in a chorus of bravos. For my mother – who, as I have already pointed out, was a pathetic cook – also served us mayonnaise, and quite often at that, although her mayonnaise came in a glass jar from the supermarket; despite this insult to truly discerning taste, it nevertheless led to an unshakeable preference. While one might mourn the tasty, homemade touch necessary to produce pure mayonnaise, processed mayonnaise offers one characteristic that is lacking in the real thing, and the best chef must, sooner or later, concede the bitter truth: even the most homogeneous and unctuous of condiments tends, very quickly, to break up a bit, slowly disintegrating, oh, only ever so slightly, but nevertheless enough for the consistency of the cream to be marred by a very slight contrast, which will cause it to abandon, in the most microscopic way, its initial state, which was utterly and absolutely smooth, as smooth as can be – whereas supermarket mayonnaise avoids any viscosity. There is no texture, there are no elements, no components, and that is what I loved passionately, that taste of nothing, that substance without backbone, offering no hold with which to circumvent it as it slid along my tongue with the fluidity of something soluble.

Yes, that's it, that's nearly it. Between the breast of Peking duck and the ointment in a jar, between the lair of a genius and the grocery shelves, I would choose the latter, I would choose the horrid little supermarket where the guilty objects of my delight were lined up in dreary, uniform rows. The supermarket . . . Odd how this is stirring a wave of emotion . . . Yes, perhaps . . . perhaps . . .

Rue de Grenelle, the Corridor

S uch a waste.

He has crushed everything in his wake. Everything. His children, his wife, his mistresses, even his own creative work: now in his final hours he is rejecting it all, because of this request that he himself does not understand, but which is tantamount to a condemnation of his science and a denunciation of everything he once stood for, a request he has addressed to us like a beggar, like a ragged pauper by the roadside, deprived of any meaningful life, alienated from his own understanding – wretched, in the end, because he has realised, in this moment among all others, that he has been chasing a chimera and preaching a false gospel. A flavour . . . What do you think, you old madman, what do you think? That if you find a lost flavour you will eradicate decades of misunderstanding and find yourself confronted with a truth that might redeem the aridity of your heart of stone? And yet he had in his possession all the arms that make for the best duellist: a fine way with his pen, nerve, panache. His prose . . . his prose was nectar, ambrosia, a hymn to language: it was gut-wrenching, and it hardly mattered whether he was talking about food or something else, it would be a mistake to think that the topic mattered: it was the way he phrased it that was so brilliant. Food was just a pretext, perhaps even a way of escaping, of fleeing what his goldsmith's talent might bring to light: the exact tenor of his emotions, the harshness and suffering, and the failure, in the end . . . Thus, where his genius might have enabled him to dissect for posterity and for himself the various feelings which were troubling him, he lost his way along secondary paths, convinced that he ought to say what was incidental, and not essential. Such a waste. Heartbreaking.

And as for me . . . obsessed as he was with his sham success, he did not see who I really am. Neither the striking contrast between my ambitions as a young hothead and the life as a quiet notable that I lead against my will; nor my stubborn tendency to muddle our conversation, to hide the inhibitions of a sad childhood beneath a ceremonial cynicism, to join him in performing a farce that may have seemed brilliant but was really nothing more than an illusion. Paul, the prodigal nephew, the favourite child – favourite because he had dared to refuse, dared to break the tyrant's laws, dared to speak loud and clear in his presence where others whispered: but, old madman, even the most turbulent, even the most violent, the most rebellious of sons cannot be all those things without the formal authorisation of the father, and yet again it is the father who, for a reason unbeknownst to himself, *needs* this trouble-maker, needs to have this spine planted in the heart of his home, needs this small refuge of opposition, a place where, in the end, all the oversimplified categories of will and character shall be proven wrong. I was your henchman for the simple reason that it was what you wanted, and how many sensible young men could have resisted such a temptation – to become the flattered foil to a universal demiurge, taking on the role of opponent that he had created specially for them? Old madman, old madman . . . You scorn Jean, you praise me to the skies, and yet we are both little more than the product of your desire – with the only difference that Jean is dying because of it, whereas I delight in it and make the most of it.

But it is too late now, too late to speak truthfully, to save what might have been saved. I am not enough of a Christian to believe in conversion, let alone last-minute conversion, and for my expiation I will live with the burden of my cowardice, that of having played at being what I am not, until for me, too, death ensues.

I'll speak to Jean all the same.

The Illumination

Rue de Grenelle, the Bedroom

Then suddenly I remember. Tears flow from my eyes. I murmur frenetically a few words incomprehensible to those around me, I am weeping and laughing at the same time, I raise my arms and trace circles convulsively with my hands. Around me everyone is agitated, concerned. I know I must look like what I am, basically: a mature man on his deathbed, who has lapsed into infancy as he prepares to depart his life. With a Dantean effort I manage to restrain my excitement for a short spell – a titanic struggle against my own jubilation, because I absolutely must make myself clear.

'My . . . little . . . Paul,' I manage to utter, with difficulty, 'my . . . little . . . Paul . . . do . . . something . . . for . . . me.'

He is leaning over me, his nose almost touching mine; his brows, frowning with anxiety, form an admirable motif around his distraught blue eyes, and his entire body is tense with the effort to understand me.

'Yes, yes, Uncle,' he says. 'What do you want, what do you want?'

'Go and . . . buy me . . . some . . . chouquettes,' I say, realising with horror that the exultation flooding my soul as I utter these marvellous words could usher me brutally out of this world before it is time. I stiffen, expecting the worst, but nothing happens. I catch my breath.

'Chouquettes? You want some chouquettes?'

I nod, smiling faintly. A trace of a smile forms gently on his sour lips.

'So that's what you want, you old madman, some chouquettes?' He squeezes my arm affectionately. 'I'll go and get some. I'll go right away.'

I can see Anna behind him, coming to life, and I hear her say, 'Go to Lenôtre, it's the closest.'

A cramp of terror seizes my heart. As in the worst nightmares, the words seem to take an endless amount of time just to come out of my mouth, whereas the movements of the human beings around me accelerate with dizzying speed. I can sense that Paul will vanish around the door before my words make it into the open air – the air of my salvation, the air of my final redemption. So I move, gesticulate, throw my pillow to the floor and, oh infinite mercy, oh miracle of the gods, oh ineffable relief, they turn to look at me.

'What is it, Uncle?'

In two steps – however do they manage to be so nimble, so quick, I must already be in another world, where they seem to me to be seized by the same frenetic gestures as in the earliest silent films, when actors had the accelerated, jerky gestures of dementia – my nephew is once again within earshot. I hiccup with relief, I can see him go tense with worry, I reassure them with a pitiful gesture while Anna hurries to pick up the pillow.

'Not . . . Lenôtre,' I croak, 'anything . . . but . . . Lenôtre . . . Not . . . a . . . patisserie . . . I . . . want . . . choux . . . in . . . a . . . plastic . . . bag . . . from . . . Leclerc.' I gasp for breath. 'Soft . . . choux . . . I . . . want . . . supermarket . . . choux . . .'

And while I penetrate deep into his gaze, filling my own with all the strength of my desire and despair – because this is, for the first time quite literally, a question of life or death – I see that he has understood. I sense it, I know it. He nods, and in his nod a fleeting reminiscence of our former complicity is painfully reborn, with a pain that is joyful, calming. I need no longer speak. As he leaves, almost at a run, I let myself slide into the cottony bliss of memory.

They were waiting for me, in their transparent plastic bag. On the wooden display, alongside the wrapped baguettes, whole-wheat breads, brioches and flans: the little bags of chouquettes, waiting patiently. Because they'd been tossed there, higgledy-piggledy, with no respect for the art of the pâtissier which would have had them lovingly arranged, with plenty of room, on a display in front of the counter, they stuck together at the bottom of the bag, squeezed one against the other like sleeping puppies in the tranquil warmth of the fray. Above all, they had been set all warm and steamy in their final resting place, giving off a decisive steam which, when it condensed on the sides of the bag, created an environment conducive to sogginess.

The criteria that go into any great chouquette are those of any self-respecting choux pastry. One must avoid softening and chewiness in equal measure. The consistency of the choux must be neither elastic nor limp, neither brittle nor aggressively dry. Their glory stems from an ability to be tender without being frail, and firm without being stiff. It is incumbent upon pâtissiers who fill choux with cream to avoid contaminating the filled choux with sogginess. I have already written vengeful and devastating pieces on those choux that utterly went off the rails, sumptuous pages on the capital importance of borders where choux à la crème are concerned – and on bad choux, the ones that can no longer be distinguished from the butter seeping from within, their identity lost in the indolence of a substance to which they should, however, have opposed the perennial nature of their difference. Or something to that effect.

How can one betray oneself to such a degree? What corruption greater even than power can lead us to thus deny the proof of pleasure, to hold in contempt that which we have loved, to defile our own taste to such a degree? I was fifteen years old, I had just left the lycée for the day, famished the way one often is at that age, without discernment, quite wildly and yet with a tranquillity that I recall only today, and that is precisely what is so cruelly lacking in my entire *oeuvre*. My entire *oeuvre* – I would give it all this evening without regret, without a shadow of remorse or a smidgeon of nostalgia, for one single, final chouquette from the supermarket.

I opened the bag carelessly, yanked on the plastic and then tore coarsely at the hole my impatience had created. I thrust my hand into the bag, and I didn't like the sticky contact with the sugar that condensation had left on the sides of the bag. Painstakingly I detached one chouquette from its fellows, carried it religiously to my mouth and swallowed it down, closing my eyes.

Much has been written about the first bite, the second, and the third. Many worthy things have been professed on the subject. All are true. But they do not attain, far from it, the ineffable nature of that sensation, of lightly touching then gradually crushing the moist batter in a mouth that has become orgasmic. The sugar had soaked in moisture and did not crunch; it crystallised as you bit into it, its particles broke up without violence, harmoniously, your jaws did not break the sugar, but scattered it gently, in an indescribable waltz of creamy and crunchy. The chouquette clung to the most secret membranes of my palate, its sensual softness embraced my cheeks, its indecent elasticity caused it to congeal immediately in a homogeneous and unctuous paste which the sweetness of the sugar enhanced with a hint of perfection. I swallowed it quickly, because there were nineteen more to explore. Only the last chouquettes would be chewed and chewed again with the despair of the imminent end. I found consolation in musing about the last offering of the divine little pouch: the crystals of sugar that remained at the very bottom, waiting for choux to cling to; using my sticky fingers, I would fill the last little magical spheres with this sugar, to conclude my feast in an explosion of sweetness.

*

In the almost mystical union between my tongue and these supermarket chouquettes, with their industrial batter and their treacly sugar, I attained God. Since then, I have lost him, sacrificed him to the glorious desires which were not mine and which, in the twilight of my life, have very nearly succeeded in concealing him from me again.

God – that is, raw, unequivocal pleasure, the pleasure which stems from our innermost core, cares for nothing other than our own delight, and returns to it in like fashion; God – that is, that mysterious region in our most secret self with which we are completely in tune in the apotheosis of authentic desire and unadulterated pleasure. Like the umbilicus nestled in our deepest phantasms, which only our deepest self can inspire, chouquettes were the assumption of my life strength, of my power to exist. I could have written about chouquettes my whole life long; and my whole life long, I wrote against them. It is only in the instant of my death that I have found them again, after so many years of wandering. And it matters little, in the end, whether Paul brings them to me before I expire.

The question is not one of eating, nor is it one of living; the question is knowing why. In the name of the father, the son, and the chouquette, amen. I die.

Thanks to Pierre Gagnaire, for the menu and for his poetry.

For discussion

How far do you think *The Gourmet* is a book of the senses?

Muriel Barbery's writing evokes food very vividly. Which was your favourite description of food and why?

Pierre Arthens has ruthlessly pursued ambition and personal enjoyment at the expense of everyone else in his life. What do you think drove him to do this? Do you think it is a trait shared by many people who achieve this level of success?

Is there anything surprising about Arthens's personality? Do you find him at all likeable? Why does he seem to have a special affinity with animals?

There are many memories of childhood in the book. Which would you say best captures how children experience the world?

How significant is the theme of self-deception in the story?

What does the book tell us about the difference between the way individuals present themselves to the world and how they feel inside?

How do the many voices who speak in the novel contribute to our understanding of Arthens? Do you feel this is an effective way of telling the story?

What did you think of the ending? What does Arthens derive from finally remembering his long-sought-after flavour?

Ultimately, is the book really about the significance of food?

Extract from *The Elegance of the Hedgehog.*
Published in B format June 2009.
ISBN 978-1-906040-18-5
£7.99

The Miracles of Art

My name is Renée. I am fifty-four years old. For twenty-seven years I have been the concierge at number 7, Rue de Grenelle, a fine *hôtel particulier* with a courtyard and private gardens, divided into eight luxury apartments, all of which are inhabited, all of which are immense. I am a widow, I am short, ugly and plump, I have bunions on my feet and, if I am to credit certain early mornings of self-inflicted disgust, the breath of a mammoth. I did not go to university, I have always been poor, discreet and insignificant. I live alone with my cat, a big lazy tom who has no distinguishing features other than the fact that his paws smell bad when he is annoyed. Neither he nor I make any effort to take part in the social doings of our respective species. Because I am rarely friendly – though always polite – I am not liked, but am tolerated nonetheless: I correspond so very well to what social prejudice has collectively construed to be a typical French concierge that I am one of the multiple cogs that make the great universal illusion turn, the illusion according to which life has a meaning that can be easily deciphered. And since it has been written somewhere that concierges are old, ugly and sour, so has it been branded in fiery letters on the pediment of that same imbecilic firmament that the afore mentioned concierges have rather large dithering cats who sleep all day on cushions covered with crocheted cases.

Similarly, it has been decreed that concierges watch television interminably while their rather large cats doze, and that the entrance to the building must smell of pot-au-feu, cabbage soup or a country-style cassoulet. I have the extraordinary good fortune to be the concierge of a very high-class sort of building. It was so humiliating for me to have to cook such loathsome dishes that when Monsieur de Broglie – the State Councillor on the first floor – intervened (an intervention he described to his wife as being 'courteous but firm', whose only intention was to rid our communal habitat of such plebeian effluvia), it came as an immense relief, one I concealed as best I could beneath an expression of reluctant compliance.

That was twenty-seven years ago. Since then, I have gone every day to the butcher's to buy a slice of ham or some calves' liver, which I slip into my net bag between my packet of noodles and my bunch of carrots. I then obligingly flaunt these pauper's victuals – now much improved by the noteworthy fact that they do not smell – because I am a pauper in a house full of rich people and this display nourishes both the consensual cliché and my cat Leo, who has become rather large by virtue of these meals that should have been mine, and who stuffs himself liberally and noisily with macaroni and butter, and pork from the delicatessen, while I am free – without any olfactory disturbances or anyone suspecting a thing – to indulge my own culinary proclivities.

Far more irksome was the issue of the television. In my late husband's day, I did go along with it, for the constancy of his viewing spared me the chore of watching. From the hallway of the building you could hear the sound of the thing, and that sufficed to perpetuate the charade of social hierarchy, but once Lucien had passed away I had to think hard to find a way to keep up appearances. Alive, he freed me from this iniquitous obligation; dead, he has deprived me of his lack of culture, the indispensable bulwark against other people's suspicions.

I found a solution thanks to a non-buzzer.

A chime linked to an infrared mechanism now alerts me to the comings and goings in the hallway, which has eliminated the need for anyone to buzz to notify me of their presence if I happen to be out of earshot. For on such occasions I am actually in the back room, where I spend most of my hours of leisure and where, sheltered from the noise and smells that my condition imposes, I can live as I please, without being deprived of the information vital to any sentry: who is coming in, who is going out, with whom and at what time.

Thus, the residents going down the hall would hear the muffled sounds indicating a television was on, and as they tend to lack rather than abound in imagination, they would form a mental image of the concierge sprawled in front of her television set. As for me, cosily installed in my lair, I heard nothing but I knew that someone was going by. So I would go to the adjacent room and peek through the spy-hole located opposite the stairs and, well hidden behind the white net curtains, I could enquire discreetly as to the identity of the passer-by.

With the advent of videocassettes and, subsequently, the DVD divinity, things changed radically, much to the enrichment of my happy hours. As it is not terribly common to come across a concierge waxing ecstatic over *Death in Venice* or to hear strains of Mahler wafting from her lodge, I delved into my hard-earned conjugal savings and bought a second television set that I could operate in my hideaway. Thus, the television in the front room, guardian of my clandestine activities, could bleat away and I was no longer forced to listen to inane nonsense fit for the brain of a clam – I was in the back room, perfectly euphoric, my eyes filling with tears, in the miraculous presence of Art.

Profound Thought No. 1

Follow the stars
In the goldfish bowl
An end

A pparently, now and again adults take the time to sit down and contemplate what a disaster their life is. They complain without understanding and, like flies constantly banging against the same old windowpane, they buzz around, suffer, waste away, get depressed then wonder how they got caught up in this spiral that is taking them where they don't want to go. The most intelligent among them turn their malaise into a religion: oh, the despicable vacuousness of bourgeois existence! Cynics of this kind frequently dine at Papa's table: 'What has become of the dreams of our youth?' they ask, with a smug, disillusioned air. 'Those years are long gone, and life's a bitch.' I despise this false lucidity that comes with age. The truth is that they are just like everyone else: nothing more than kids who don't understand what has happened to them, acting big and tough when in fact all they want is to burst into tears.

And yet there's nothing to understand. The problem is that children believe what adults say and, once they're adults themselves, they exact their revenge by deceiving their own children. 'Life has meaning and we grown-ups know what it is' is the universal lie that everyone is supposed to believe. Once you become an adult and you realise that's not true, it's too late. The mystery remains intact, but all your available energy has long ago been wasted on stupid things. All that's left is to anaes-thetise yourself by trying to hide the fact that you can't find any meaning in your life, and then, the better to convince yourself, you deceive your own children.

All our family acquaintances have followed the same path: their youth spent trying to make the most of their intelligence, squeezing their studies like a lemon to make sure they'd secure a spot among the elite, then the rest of their lives wondering with a flabbergasted look on their faces why all that hopefulness has led to such a vain existence. People aim for the stars, and they end up like goldfish in a bowl. I wonder if it wouldn't be simpler just to teach children right from the start that life is absurd. That might deprive you of a few good moments in your childhood but it would save you a considerable amount of time as an adult − not to mention the fact that you'd be spared at least one traumatic experience, i.e. the goldfish bowl.

I am twelve years old, I live at 7, Rue de Grenelle in an apartment for rich people. My parents are rich, my family is rich and my sister and I are, therefore, as good as rich. My father is a member of parliament and before that he was a minister: no doubt he'll end up in the top spot, emptying out the wine cellar of the residence at the Hôtel de Lassay. As for my mother . . . Well, my mother isn't exactly a genius but she is educated. She has a literature PhD. She writes her dinner invitations without mistakes and spends her time bombarding us with literary references ('Colombe, stop trying to act like Madame Guermantes,' or 'Sweetie, you are a regular Sanseverina').

Despite all that, despite all this good fortune and all this wealth, I have known for a very long time that the final destination is the goldfish bowl. How do I know? Well, the fact is I am very intelligent. Exceptionally intelligent, in fact. Even now, if you look at children my age, there's an abyss between us. And since I don't really want to stand out, and since

6

intelligence is very highly rated in my family – an exceptionally gifted child would never have a moment's peace – I try to scale back my performance at school, but even so I always come first. You might think that to pretend to be simply of average intelligence when you are twelve years old like me and have the level of a second-year university student is easy. Well, not at all. It really takes an effort to appear stupider than you are. But, in a way, this does keep me from dying of boredom: all the time I don't need to spend learning and understanding I use to imitate the ordinary good pupils – the way they do things, the answers they give, their progress, their concerns and their minor errors. I read everything that Constance Baret writes – she is second in the class – all her maths and French and history and that way I find out what I have to do: for French a string of words that are coherent and spelled correctly; for maths the mechanical reproduction of operations devoid of meaning; and for history a list of events joined by logical connections. But even if you compare me to an adult, I am much brighter than the vast majority. That's the way it is. I'm not particularly proud of this because it's not my doing. But one thing is certain – there's no way I'm going to end up in the goldfish bowl. I've thought this through quite carefully. Even for someone like me who is superbright and gifted in her studies and different from everyone else, in fact superior to the vast majority – even for me life is already all plotted out and so dismal you could cry: no one seems to have thought of the fact that if life is absurd, being a brilliant success has no greater value than being a failure. It's just more comfortable. And even then: I think lucidity gives your success a bitter taste, whereas mediocrity still leaves hope for something.

So I've made up my mind. I am about to leave childhood behind and, in spite of my conviction that life is a farce, I don't think I can hold out to the end. We are, basically, programmed to believe in something that doesn't exist, because we are living creatures; we don't want to suffer. So we spend all our energy persuading ourselves that there are things that are worthwhile and that that is why life has meaning. I may be very intelligent, but I don't know how much longer I'm going to be able to struggle against this biological tendency. When I join the adults in the rat race, will I still be able to confront this feeling of absurdity? I don't think so. That is why I've made up my mind: at the end of the school year, on the day I turn thirteen, the sixteenth of June, I will commit suicide.

An Aristocrat

On Tuesdays and Thursdays, Manuela, my only friend, comes for tea with me in my lodge. Manuela is a simple woman and twenty years wasted stalking dust in other people's homes has in no way robbed her of her elegance. Besides, stalking dust is a very euphemistic way to put it. But where the rich are concerned, things are rarely called by their true name.

'I empty bins full of sanitary towels,' she says, with her gentle, slightly hissing accent. 'I wipe up dog vomit, clean the bird cage – you'd never believe the amount of poo such tiny animals can make – and I scrub the toilets. You talk about dust? Big deal!'

You must understand that when she comes down to see me at two in the afternoon, on Tuesdays after the Arthens, and on Thursdays after the de Broglies, Manuela has been polishing the toilets with a cotton bud, and though they may be gilded with gold leaf, they are just as filthy and reeking as any toilets on the planet, because if there is one thing the rich do share with the poor, however unwillingly, it is their nauseating intestines that always manage to find a place to free themselves of that which makes them stink.

So Manuela deserves our praise. Although she's been sacrificed at the altar of a world where the most thankless tasks have been allotted to some women while others merely hold their nose without raising a finger, she nevertheless strives relentlessly to maintain a degree of refinement that goes far beyond any gold-leaf gilding, *a fortiori* of the sanitary variety.

'When you eat a walnut, you must use a tablecloth,' says

Manuela, removing from her old shopping bag a little hamper made of light wood where some almond *tuiles* are nestled among curls of carmine tissue paper. I make coffee that we shall not drink, but its wafting aroma delights us both, and in silence we sip a cup of green tea as we nibble on our tuiles.

Just as I am a permanent traitor to my archetype, so is Manuela: to the Portuguese cleaning woman she is a criminal oblivious of her condition. This girl from Faro, born under a fig tree after seven siblings and before six more, forced in childhood to work the fields and scarcely out of it to marry a mason and take the road of exile, mother of four children who are French by birthright but whom society looks upon as thoroughly Portuguese – this girl from Faro, as I was saying, who wears the requisite black support stockings and a kerchief on her head, is an aristocrat. An authentic one, of the kind whose entitlement you cannot contest: it is etched onto her very heart, it mocks titles and people with handles to their names. What is an aristocrat? A woman who is never sullied by vulgarity, although she may be surrounded by it.

On Sundays, the vulgarity of her in-laws, who with their loud laughter muffle the pain of being born weak and without prospects; the vulgarity of an environment as bleakly desolate as the neon lights of the factory where the men go each morning, like sinners returning to hell; then, the vulgarity of her employers who, for all their money, cannot hide their own baseness and who speak to her the way they would a mangy dog covered with oozing bald patches. But you should have witnessed Manuela offering me, as if I were a queen, the fruit of her prowess in *haute pâtisserie* to fully appreciate the grace that inhabits this woman. Yes, as if I were a queen. When Manuela arrives, my lodge is transformed into a palace, and a picnic between two pariahs becomes the feast of two monarchs. Like a storyteller transforming life into a shimmering river where trouble and boredom vanish far below the water, Manuela metamorphoses our existence into a warm and joyful epic.

'That little Pallières boy said hello to me on the stairs,' she says suddenly, interrupting the silence.

I snort with disdain.

'He's reading Marx,' I add, with a shrug of my shoulders.

'Marx?' she asks, pronouncing the *x* as if it were a *sh*, a somewhat slurping *sh*, as charming as a clear sky.

'The father of communism,' I reply.

Manuela makes a scornful noise.

'Politics,' she says. 'A toy for little rich kids that they won't let anyone else play with.'

She is thoughtful for a moment, frowning.

'Not his typical reading material,' she says.

The illustrated magazines that the young boys hide under the mattress cannot escape Manuela's shrewd gaze, and the Pallières boy seemed at one point to be consuming them assiduously, however selectively, as exemplified by one particularly dog-eared page with an explicit title: *The Saucy Marchionesses*.

We laugh and converse for a while longer about one thing or another, in the calm space of an old friendship. These are precious moments for me, and I am filled with anguish at the thought that a day will come when Manuela will fulfil her lifelong dream of returning to her country for good, and will leave me here alone and decrepit, with no companion to transform me, twice a week, into a clandestine monarch. I also wonder fearfully what will happen when the only friend I have ever had, the only one who knows everything without ever having to ask, leaves behind her this woman whom no one knows, enshrouding her in oblivion.

Profound Thought No. 2

The cat here on earth
Modern totem
And intermittently decorative

n any case, this is true at our place. If you want to understand my family, all you have to do is look at the cats. Our two cats are fat windbags who eat designer cat food and have no interesting interaction with human beings. They drag themselves from one sofa to the next and leave their fur everywhere, and no one seems to have grasped that they have no affection for any of us. The only purpose of cats is that they constitute mobile decorative objects, a concept which I find intellectually interesting, but unfortunately, our cats have such drooping bellies that this does not apply to them.

My mother, who has read all of Balzac and quotes Flaubert at every dinner, is living proof every day of how education is a raging fraud. All you need to do is watch her with the cats. She's vaguely aware of their decorative potential, and yet she insists on talking to them as if they were people, which she would never do with a lamp or an Etruscan statue. It would seem that children believe for a fairly long time that anything that moves has a soul and is endowed with intention. My mother is no longer a child but she apparently has not managed to conceive that Constitution and Parliament possess no more understanding than the vacuum cleaner. I concede that the difference between the vacuum cleaner and the cats is that a cat can experience pain and pleasure. But does that mean it has a greater ability to communicate with humans? Not at all. That should simply incite us to take special precautions with them as we would with very fragile objects. When I hear my mother say, 'Constitution is both a very proud and very sensitive little cat,' when in fact said cat is sprawled on the sofa because she's eaten too much, it really makes me want to laugh. But if you think about the hypothesis that a cat's purpose is to act as a modern totem, a sort of emblematic incarnation, protector of the home, reflecting well upon its owners, then everything becomes clear. My mother makes the cats into what she wishes we were, and which we absolutely are not. You won't find anyone less proud and sensitive than the three aforementioned members of the Josse family: Papa, Maman and Colombe. They are utterly spineless and anaesthetised, emptied of all emotion.

In short, in my opinion the cat is a modern totem. Say what you want, do what you will with all those fine speeches on evolution, civilisation and a ton of other '-tion' words, mankind has not progressed very far from its origins: people still believe they're not here by chance, and that there are gods, kindly for the most part, who are watching over their fate.

Red October

By Christmas 1989 Lucien was very sick. We did not yet know when his death would come, but we were bound by the certainty of its imminence, bound to the dread inside, bound to each other by these invisible ties. When illness enters a home, not only does it take hold of a body; it also weaves a dark web between hearts, a web where hope is trapped. Like a spider's thread drawn ever tighter around our plans, making it impossible to breathe, with each passing day the illness was overwhelming our life. When I came in from running chores outside, it was like entering a dark cellar where I was constantly cold, with a chill that nothing could remedy, so much so towards the end that when I slept alongside Lucien, it seemed as if his body were sucking up all the heat my body might have managed to purloin elsewhere.

His illness was first diagnosed in the spring of 1988; it ate away at him for seventeen months and carried him off just before Christmas. The elder Madame Meurisse organised a collection from among the inhabitants of the building, and a fine wreath of flowers was delivered to my lodge, bound with a ribbon that bore no text. She alone came to the funeral. She was a cold, stiff, pious woman, but there was something sincere about her austere and rather abrupt manner, and when she died, a year after Lucien, I said to myself that she had been a good woman and that I would miss her, although we had scarcely exchanged two words in fifteen years.

'She made her daughter-in-law miserable right up to the end. May she rest in peace, she was a saintly woman,' said Manuela – who professes a truly epic hatred for the younger Madame Meurisse – by way of a funeral oration.

Thus with the exception of Cornélia Meurisse, with her little veils and rosaries, Lucien's illness did not strike anyone as being worthy of interest. To rich people it must seem that the ordinary little people – perhaps because their lives are more impoverished, deprived of the oxygen of money and savoir-faire – experience human emotions with less intensity and greater indifference. Since we were concierges, it was a given that death, for us, must be a matter of course, whereas for our privileged neighbours it carried all the weight of injustice and drama. The death of a concierge leaves a slight indentation on everyday life, belongs to a biological certainty that has nothing tragic about it and, for the apartment owners who encountered him every day on the stairs or at the door to our lodge, Lucien was a nonentity who was merely returning to a nothingness from which he had never fully emerged, a creature who, because he had lived only half a life, with neither luxury nor artifice, must at the moment of his death have felt no more than half a shudder of revolt. The fact that we might be going through hell like any other human being, or that our hearts might be filling with rage as Lucien's suffering ravaged our lives, or that we might be slowly going to pieces inside, in the torment of fear and horror that death inspires in everyone, did not cross the mind of anyone on these premises.

One morning three weeks before that Christmas, I had just come in from shopping with a bag filled with turnips and lung for the cat, and there was Lucien dressed and ready to go out. He had even knotted his scarf and was standing there waiting for me. After weeks of witnessing my husband's agony as, drained of all strength and enveloped in a terrifying pallor, he would hobble from the bedroom to the kitchen; after weeks of seeing him wear nothing other than a pair of pyjamas that looked the very uniform of demise, and now to find him with his eyes shining and a mischievous expression on his face, the collar of his winter coat turned right up to his peculiarly pink cheeks: I very nearly collapsed.

'Lucien!' I exclaimed, and I was about to go to hold him up, sit him down, undress him and I don't know what else, everything that the illness had taught me in the way of unfamiliar gestures, which had become of late the only ones I knew how to make. I was about to put my bag down and embrace him, hold him close to me, carry him, all those things once more, when, breathless and feeling a strange flutter of expansion in my heart, I stopped in my tracks.

'We'll just make it,' said Lucien, 'the next showing is at one.'

In the heat of the cinema, on the verge of tears, happier than I had ever been, I was holding the faint warmth of his hand for the first time in months. I knew that an unexpected surge of energy had roused him from his bed, given him the strength to get dressed and the urge to go out, the desire for us to share a conjugal pleasure one more time – and I knew, too, that this was the sign that there was not much time left, a state of grace before the end. But that did not matter to me, I just wanted to make the most of it, of these moments stolen from the burden of illness, moments with his warm hand in mine and a shudder of pleasure going through both of us because, thank heavens, it was a film we could share and delight in equally.

I think he died right after that. His body held on for three more weeks, but his mind departed at the end of the film, because he knew it was better that way, because he had said farewell to me in the darkened cinema. There were no poignant regrets, because he had found peace this way; he had placed his trust in what we had said to each other without any need for words, while we watched, together, the bright screen where a story was being told.

And I accepted it.

The Hunt for Red October is the film of our last embrace. For anyone who wants to understand the art of storytelling, this film should suffice; one wonders why universities persist in teaching narrative principles on the basis of Propp, Greimas or other such punishing curricula, instead of investing in a projection room. Premise, plot, protagonists, adventures, quest, heroes and other stimulants: all you need is Sean Connery in the uniform of a Russian submarine officer and a few well-placed aircraft carriers.

This morning on France Inter Radio I learned that this contamination of my aspiration to high culture by my penchant for lower forms of culture does not necessarily represent the indelible mark of my lowly origins or of my solitary striving for enlightenment but is, rather, a contemporary characteristic of the dominant intellectual class. How did I come to know this? From the mouth of a sociologist, and I would have loved to have known if he himself would have loved to have known that a concierge in Scholl clogs had just made him into a holy icon. As part of a study on the evolution of the cultural practices of intellectuals who had once been immersed in highbrow culture from dawn to dusk but who were now mainstays of syncretism in whom the boundaries between high and low culture were irreversibly blurred, my sociologist described a classics professor who, once upon a time, would have listened to Bach, read Mauriac, and watched art-house films, but nowadays listened to Handel and MC Solaar, read Flaubert and John Le Carré, went to see Visconti and the latest *Die Hard,* and ate hamburgers at lunch and sashimi in the evening.

How distressing to stumble on a dominant social habitus, just when one was convinced of one's own uniqueness in the matter! Distressing, and perhaps even a bit annoying. The fact that, in spite of my confinement in a lodge that conforms in every way to what is expected, in spite of an isolation that should have protected me from the imperfections of the masses, in spite of those shameful years in my forties when I

17

was utterly ignorant of the changes in the vast world to which I am confined; the fact that I, Renée, fifty-four years old, concierge and autodidact, am witness to the same changes that are animating the present-day elite – the little Pallières in their exclusive schools who read Marx then go off in gangs to watch *Terminator,* or the little Badoises who study law at Assas and sob into their Kleenex at *Notting Hill* – is a shock from which I can scarcely recover. And it is patently clear, for those who pay attention to chronology, that I am not the one who is aping these youngsters but, rather, in my eclectic practices, I am well ahead of them.

Renée, prophet of the contemporary elite.

'And well, why not,' I thought, removing the cat's slice of calves' liver from my shopping bag, and from beneath that, carefully wrapped in an unmarked sheet of plastic, two little fillets of red mullet which I intend to marinate then cook in lemon juice and coriander.

And this is when it all started.